# Tommy Gunz

## PART TWO

## Warren Holloway

*AMERICA'S NEW STORYTELLER*

D0111759

**GOOD 2 GO PUBLISHING**

**ALL EYES ON GUNZ 2**

Written by Warren Holloway

Cover Design: Davida Baldwin – Odd Ball Designs

Typesetter: Mychea

ISBN: 9781947340282

Copyright © 2018 Good2Go Publishing

Published 2018 by Good2Go Publishing

7311 W. Glass Lane • Laveen, AZ 85339

www.good2gopublishing.com

https://twitter.com/good2gobooks

G2G@good2gopublishing.com

www.facebook.com/good2gopublishing

www.instagram.com/good2gopublishing

# CHAPTER 1

*One Year Later*

I WAS IN ATLANTA loving the city and its women. The black sistas down here all seemed to be exotic in one way or another, plus the strippers took it to a whole another level. They were getting money for real. Their whips were hotter than some of the niggas' out here. The summer was closing in, so all of the sexy-ass ATL women would be out looking the part. Like most cities, the ballas also came out showing their status as well, with diamonds, cars, watches, and clothing. They were all stunting for real.

I had a sky-blue Range Rover HSE Sport with chrome 24-inch Antars and custom white leather seats piped in sky blue. This was my toy to run around in the city. Right now, I was on my way back to the Thomasville projects, bumping to Young Jeezy's Inspiration CD. This shit was hustla music for real. If you weren't getting it, this would make you go get it. As I drove into the projects, my wrist on ice was hanging out the window, showing off yellow and white diamonds that were sparkling under the sun. My PA swag was on ten with my sky-blue Jordan 23 jersey and shorts flowing with my Air Force Ones. It was my Monday look. My music was blasting loud with the Atlanta native flowing over the beat that was inspiring all go-gettas.

This city had taken to me, especially the little homies from this project. They were feeling my gangsta and knowing how real I was and what my story was. I managed to put a crew together, too. These little niggas saw me pulling into the projects, so they started walking up to my truck as I slowed before coming to a stop. Yeah, the money I brought down here I just flipped it to get the local numbers from Mr. 17-5 himself. I made do with what was available. Besides, up until this point, I couldn't do too much. One thing

I did know how to do well was build my own empire.

As my little homies were greeting me and paying me the money they owed, the hood was coming alive as these two bitches started arguing and fighting. Shit like this drew heat on the projects, and we couldn't have that because we were getting money out here.

"Yo, somebody break that shit up!" I yelled out.

"Yeah, them hoes trippin'!" Ra Ra said before making his way over to the chicks with Fat Money.

Both of them were my little homies, along with Little D and Geez. These ATL niggas were the realest, plus they were about the money and didn't take shit.

I turned to put the money the homies gave me into my truck, and then I turned the music down to focus more on the business at hand. Right then the hood came alive as a roaring gunshot sounded off. I immediately reached on the side of my armrest and grabbed my nickel-plated .44mm Magnum snub nose, with two speed loaders. One of these slugs alone would take a nigga out, and the rest would run or take cover once they heard the loudness of it.

I could hear Little D and Geez yelling. It just wasn't clear what they were saying, but I was about to find out.

Little D, Geez, Ra, and Fat Money all grew up in Thomasville Projects, so they were like brothers from another mother.

Geez was carrying a Glock 40mm while Little D had twin nickel-plated .380s with pearl handles. Ra Ra was standing with his 9mm out and pointing it at the two chicks that were fighting, plus this nigga that they were fighting over. As I came up fast with my Magnum in hand, I noticed Fat Money wasn't standing, which meant shit was about to go down.

"What the fuck is going on? Who shot my little nigga?" I asked, ready to put someone down about this, especially shooting him over these bitches.

Fat Money had been shot in the leg and shoulder.

"That muthafucka right there hit over these bitches!" Fat Money said.

The females were fighting over this cat that shot Fat Money.

"See, bitch, your man got all of this shit started! He should learn how to keep his dick in his pants. Then this type of shit wouldn't happen!" the opposing female said while pointing her finger in the other girl's face. "It's this bitch's fault, too."

"Get ya hand out of my face before I slap

the shit out of you!" the other female said.

"Both of y'all got my little nigga shot,

and I ain't feeling this shit!" I said, placing

the .44 Magnum to this nigga's head and

giving him a reality check. "You stupid

muthafucka! We out here getting this money,

and you want to shoot niggas over bitches!

My nigga, Fat Money, was trying to help you

get these bitches in check. But he touched yo'

bitch, so you felt a need to do this dumb shit!"

I was pissed about this shit, and this nigga

could see it in my eyes and hear it in my tone

of voice. "What's your name, little nigga?"

"My, my, my name is Ace," the young

eighteen-year-old said. He was nervous as

hell as he lowered his gun down to his side, feeling the cold steel pressing against his temple.

When he said his name, it took me back to my little cousin, Ace, up North. I took his gun from him. He didn't resist, knowing he would die.

"Give me that shit. I was going to kill you for this shit, but you and your bitches got to get out of this hood. You're not welcome here anymore. I don't care who you know in these projects. They can meet you somewhere else."

Little D, Ra Ra, and Geez looked on at this nigga and wanted to kill him. I lowered my gun while turning back to walk to my truck, when shots rang out again, followed by the screaming of the two bitches.

When I turned around quick, I saw that nigga Ace's body falling to the ground. Half of his face was missing from the slugs that violently smashed into his eyes and forced his brain and burning flesh and bones out.

"You ain't gotta kill 'em, I did!" Fat Money yelled out, making his way to his feet. "That muthafucka shouldn't have shot me."

"I guess you okay then putting in work like that?" I asked.

"These chicks wasn't even worth the slugs he got. Look at them crying like they really care," Fat Money said. "They'll forget about him in a week and be onto the next nigga."

Just as the words came out of his mouth, sirens could be heard in the distance. Normally the cops didn't bother with the projects unless calls came in heavy; and from the looks of it, they had gotten calls.

"Yo, get Fat Money out of here."

They helped him over to his old-school whip. It was a '64 Chevy with chrome spokes, two-inch white walls, butter leather, and a candy-apple-red paint job. Geez took the wheel while the others put Fat Money in the back seat.

"I can't believe we up in my car getting blood on the seats," Fat Money said. "We should have got into y'all car or something."

"You ain't fucking my shit up!" Ra Ra said.

As they took off in the car to take him to the hospital, I jumped in the Range and mashed the gas to exit the area fast. I couldn't afford to be having any encounters with the police. As for those bitches back in the projects, they were now banned from there. Plus, they wouldn't say a word to the cops. That's just how it was done in the ATL.

# CHAPTER 2

**LATER ON THAT NIGHT,** I hit up the little homie, Ra Ra, to see how Fat Money was doing.

"Big homie, what's good?" Ra Ra asked.

"Ready to get the night started, but first, how's Money doing?"

"He all right. That nigga was more concerned about the blood in his whip."

I was laughing, knowing how manicured that little fat nigga was, plus he loved his cars.

"Yo, I'm over at Foxy Lady's strip joint watching these fat asses."

"Say no more! I'm about that life, plus we got BI to talk about. You want me to bring

Geez and Little D?"

"Nah, you can come alone, my nigga."

"I'm on my way."

I was sitting in the VIP area getting a lap dance from this sexy-ass chick with a crazy body, and brown skin glowing even more with the oil and glitter flowing over her body. She had perfect, perky 36C breasts, pretty seductive hazel-brown eyes, and lips that looked like she'd keep a nigga home all day. She was shaking her ass and backing it up as Juvenile's song played. I was enjoying every bit of it, drinking on my Long Island iced tea and watching a stripper named Rain doing her thing all over me. She was working her hips, with her legs thunder clapping and more. I was feeling every bit of it watching this visual art. She was a masterpiece in motion. The song ended just as her dance did, so she turned to me.

"You want another dance?" she asked with seduction in her voice and eyes. She knew how to work it.

"I don't want another dance. I do want you to sit on my lap while I enjoy my drink."

"Time is money," she responded as if I didn't know she was all business. "I got the money if you have the time," I said while tucking two $100-dollar bills into her thong, which made her smile at the sight of the

Benjamin Franklins.

I knew she was a go-getta. She sat down with her soft ass on my lap, grinding in slow motion as she was listening to the music.

"Yo, swag is on ten, plus it's something about you," she said while still slowly grinding on me and making eye contact with them melting hazel eyes of seduction. "Where you from?"

"I'm from everywhere the money is," I responded, since it really was none of her business.

"Really? Okay," she said, turning around and mounting me as if she was naked riding me.

At the same time, she massaged my chest,

arms, and shoulders with her soft touch. She

was trying to work me, and I knew this. I had

given her some paper, but she wanted more.

I had this all under control. I knew how these

ATL strip clubs were. That was how these

broads were living so good.

I looked over at the entrance and saw Ra

Ra coming through stunting with his Atlanta

swag. The little nigga favored T.I. with his

close-cut faded on the sides. He stood five

foot eleven and weighed 160 pounds, and he

had brown skin with a baby face.

Ra Ra stopped at the bar and ordered a

double shot of Hennessy. He was representing his city with the diamond-studded ATL necklace that was flowing with the diamond bezel on the Rolex and the three-carat diamond stud in his ear.

Before he walked away from the bar, he tossed fifty ones at the stripper on the stage behind the bar, since she was working the pole and crazy popping her booty in midair.

"Damn, shawty, your ass is like Serena's!" Ra Ra said, after seeing Rain stand up and work her ass.

"You like this, huh?" she said, grabbing her own ass before making it shake and clap to twerking. She was definitely all about her ones.

"What up, little nigga?" I said, after taking a sip of my drink. "Have a seat and enjoy the views." He sat down and was still checking out Rain. "You like this?"

"You already know she got that body."

"Rain, go to the bar and get me and the homie a bottle of Moet. When you come back, give him a few dances."

I gave her $400, $300 for two bottles and the other $100 just for her.

As she turned to walk away, she blew a kiss at Ra Ra and then started walking sexy as hell in her six-inch pumps that enhanced her curves even more.

"Damn, my nigga, she special for real!"

Ra Ra said.

"Don't get T-Pained, my little homie," I said, referring to the song "I'm in Love with a Stripper"—a true classic for the strip club life and the reality of it.

Ra Ra downed the Hennessy he bought before getting into the moment and business mind-set.

"So, what's good, my nigga? What brings us here tonight?" he said.

I had to give it to this nigga. He was only twenty-one but was the sharpest of his crew. He definitely had a bright future in this game and beyond.

"I'm going to be leaving town for a few weeks, and I'm going to need you to hold it down with the BI until I get back," I said, taking a gulp of my drink. "I respect yo' gangsta and hustle. You know how to get this money. At the same time, you're not about to let anyone fuck with you or your bread. Little D, Geez, and Fat Money, they got what it takes, too, but as a leader, they'll follow you."

Ra Ra was all ears taking in every word I was dropping on him.

"I'll leave you with fifty joints and loyal clientele. Your crew will handle the rest. I'll be flying out tomorrow. Don't fuck this up, Ra Ra."

"I got you, my nigga. You ain't gotta worry about that. When it comes to this paper, I'm a get to it."

I knew he was going to handle his. It was needed for me to give him the speech. Our business talk ended when sexy-ass Rain came back with our bottles and popped the corks.

I poured her a drink from my bottle and then said, "This is a toast to my nigga, Ra Ra, and his success."

We all toasted at the same time. Then Young Jeezy's song featuring R-Kelly, "Go Getta," came on, and all of the strippers turned up. As for the bosses and ballas, they were popping bottles and feeling themselves, too. Ra Ra cupped Rain's ass and could feel the softness of her body. While at the same time, he could now feel his rise to power with me looking out for him.

Another chocolate beauty came over, seeing that this was where the money was. She's stood five foot two, with curves of perfection everywhere. She had light green eyes, a tongue ring, and one in her belly.

"What's your name, baby girl?" I asked.

"Mrs. Goodbar," she answered as she took her hand through her black, silky hair, dancing at the same time while looking sexy as a muthafucka.

ATL is definitely the home of the sistas and strippers. Both of these bad-ass chicks were dropping it low and giving me and the little homie the business as we continued to sip on the bottles of Moet.

# CHAPTER 3

**AS THE STRIPPERS CONTINUED** putting it on me and Ra Ra, I saw my phone off to the side, lighting up and signaling that I had an incoming call. I reached over past Mrs. Goodbar's fat ass and grabbed my phone.

"What's good?"

"Yo, my nigga! This is me, Sweets, my nigga. I just got hit, and I know who did this shit."

Hearing my nigga on the phone like that made me push baby girl away, so I could focus on the business at hand. This nigga, Sweets, was the first person I met when I came down this way. He was six foot three and a firm 230 pounds, with braids and a close-shaven beard lined up with the razor. This nigga also owned a rim shop over on Peach Tree Avenue.

"Sweets, where you at, my nigga?"

"Over at Club Nikki's."

"I'll be over that way ASAP," I said, hanging up the phone ready to help out the ATL homie. I turned to Ra Ra, who was all up in baby girl's ass. "Yo, playtime is over. We got shit to take care of," I said, tucking more money into Mrs. Goodbar's thong.

Normally I would take her and her girl to the hotel and get it done, but business calls.

"Let it rain, sexy girl!" Ra Ra said, tossing money in the air over the stripper, Rain.

Then he followed me out to the parking lot, knowing that it must be serious with me ending the fun we were having with them broads back there.

"What's up, big homie?"

"That nigga Sweets got robbed, and he said he knows who did this shit. We going over to where he's at now," I began. "We taking your whip."

"Say no more. Where we going?"

"Club Nikki's. I think he's over that way."

Ra Ra's M6 BMW was charcoal black with black Lexani rims and pitch-black tinted windows. This shit was a fast whip, too. Once on the highway, he opened up doing an easy one hundred without trying.

I called Sweets back to make sure he was still in position.

"Yo, my nigga, we en route right now. We going to handle this shit, all right?"

"Yeah, this shit crazy. I got caught slippin'."

"Nah, nigga. Whoever did this shit was slippin', and fucking with anybody is down with me."

Ra Ra made it to the other side of the city

fast. Being a native, he knew all of the shortcuts and back streets.

"Yo, we over by that way now."

"Them niggas must be in the club. I see the black Escalade they was in," Sweets said, all hyped up and ready to handle business.

"All right, my nigga, I see ya whip," I said and pointed at the cotton-candy-blue Chevy Impala sitting on 24s with light blue tinted windows and a white leather interior.

"Ra Ra, pull up beside the Impala."

He did just that. Sweets was just sitting there pissed.

"Yo, what they hit you for?" I asked.

"Two blocks and ten racks was what I had

28

to play with."

"How the fuck they get up on you like that?" I asked, knowing most people coming to grab heavy like that know you, because we didn't do business that heavy with too many new faces without having a proper and trusted introduction.

"This nigga Diz-lo called me up for the squares saying his man wanted them." He paused while thinking about how he trusted Diz-lo. "I'ma kill that fool Diz-lo. I did a bit with him in the Feds, so I thought he was good money. Plus, I hit him off light the other day."

I was ready to handle this shit to get the

homie's money back, plus I wanted to see how he handled himself.

"You said that's the car right there?"

"Yeah, that's they shit. I should bust all the windows out."

"All right, my nigga, we can go inside of the club or wait on them to come out."

"Let's go get 'em!"

"We going inside. Ra Ra, you stay out here and lay down anything coming through that door looking like they want war."

The plan was I was going in first. I'd sit by the stage with the strippers, and then the homie Sweets was going to come in behind me looking like he was on the dolo, which was going to make these niggas paranoid seeing him, and they'd want to leave. As I was laying down the plans for the move we were going to make on these niggas, Sweets spotted the nigga Diz-lo.

"There that nigga Diz-lo go right there," Sweets said, seeing him coming out of the club.

Diz-lo was a little nigga standing five foot three with a medium build of maybe 175 pounds. He was all about his work, but he had fucked with the wrong team.

I rolled the tinted windows back up before having Ra Ra drove slowly toward this nigga, since we were half a block away from the club's front door, because that's where Sweets parked his car. I had my .44 Magnum in hand all ready to make some noise.

Diz-lo and his homeboy were getting into the truck, ready to leave so they could go to another club and spend their newfound riches of the ten racks and two bricks. Little did they know they would never get a chance to spend it all.

Ra Ra stopped at the driver's side door. I hit the switch and rolled down the dark tinted window to reveal my face.

"Yo, little nigga," I said to get his attention as he turned my way to see who was speaking. "You is a stupid muthafucka," I said, bringing my Magnum up and quickly firing off a thunderous round into his face.

The bullet snapped his neck from the brute force of the up-close Magnum slug that was unforgiving at any range. His brains ejected out of his skull, spraying his homeboy with flesh and bones as his body slumped over on the steering wheel. His homeboy had a brief moment of shock until he snapped back into the reality of this fast-paced world. He started reaching for a gun that he put under the passenger seat before he went into the club. He took hold of it, feeling confident as he cocked it back, chambering a round to engage in fire with me. But those thoughts of shooting it out halted as slugs came through the passenger side window and pounded into his face and body, sucking the life from his flesh. I looked up to see that it was Sweets who had fired the rounds.

"Yo, check inside the truck for your shit," I said.

As he was checking for his shit, shots rang out from the steps of the club. It was another of Diz-lo's homies with a .380 that he concealed and brought into the club. He fired on Sweets after seeing that his niggas were down and dead. Plus, he knew who Sweets was.

The slugs fired from the nigga on the step

hit Sweets and dropped him. But the fear of death came fast, making his heart beat as he returned fire. He did not want to die right now. The slugs in his leg and back were burning, which only added to his pain and fear of death.

Ra Ra jumped out of his whip when he saw someone else coming out of the club. He got the MAC-10 fully automatic with a fifty clip extended from the stock. He was ready for war. He opened up fast on the nigga coming out of the club and dropped him where he stood.

Sweets fired off his last rounds at the fourth nigga that came out of the club, who acted like he really wanted it. Plus, he was one of them niggas that helped in the robbery.

Ra Ra ran up on the steps and finished off the last nigga that was still moving, but not anymore. Then he raced over to Sweets to help him up to his feet.

"Ra Ra, get the work," I said, meaning the two bricks of cocaine.

He grabbed the work after he helped Sweets to his whip. The bricks were under the passenger seat. He grabbed the joints and tossed them into the whip. He jumped into the car and mashed the gas, forcing the modified engine to thrust the car forward fast with ease. Sweets took off in his car, making his way to the hospital to get patched up. He knew he was losing blood, so he drove faster and mapped out in his head where the closest hospital was located. It seemed like the closer he got to the hospital, the farther away it became, espccially with the dizziness setting in from the loss of blood. Hc didn't realize he was closer to dying than living at this point. That reality started setting in as his vision blurred, and then it became dark. His heart slowed, and panic set in as he crashed, unable to control his car. It swerved up on the sidewalk and hit a telephone pole. He lay helpless as his life was slowly slipping away, with thoughts of how it all started with being robbed. Damn, this is for me, he started thinking as he began to feel weaker and weaker by the second, with his eyes open staring up at the sky.

"Sir, are you okay?" an old man asked, after seeing the car crash as he was walking his dog. He called 911, but Sweets was past help.

I called the nigga Sweets's phone, but it kept ringing over and over. Damn, I hoped he made it to the hospital safe. Me and Ra Ra then decided to head back over to the club to get some more visual loving from Rain and Mrs. Goodbar.

# CHAPTER 4

**IT WAS 8:00 THE** next morning and me and my little nigga, Ra Ra, sat at the Waffle House eating our cheese eggs, New York strip steaks, home fries with sautéed onions, and blueberry muffins split and fried on the grill.

I figured we'd have breakfast and go over business while I was gone. In between fucking this food up, we talked about what was needed while I was out of town.

"I want to know about anything that deviates from what we talked about. The product is in place, and you have my clientele plus the folks you already have. Little D,

Geez, and Fat Money will definitely hold you down."

"I got this, my nigga. We gonna get this paper and stack it up until you come back. Feel me?" Ra Ra said with a partial mouthful of steak and eggs. He then paused a moment in deep thought. "You know the homie died last night, too?"

"Who you talking about?"

"That boy, Sweets. He crashed out on the way to the hospital. He bled out or some shit the news was saying. The shit crazy though."

I took a moment acknowledging the loss of the homie.

"We put in all of that work last night for

him to just crash out. Damn, if I would have known that, we could have driven him to the hospital. At least he would have had a chance to be here today."

As he was talking, my eyes veered out of the window and looked on at the incoming traffic coming into the restaurant.

"What you looking at?" he asked, at the same time turning to see what I was looking at. "Oh shit, the Georgia State Troopers," Ra Ra said.

He knew that since I had been down here, this was the closest I had come in contact with the cops. I had a fake ID, plus I switched my look up a little. I just didn't like being in their way, so to speak, because even with the

fake ID, shit just might go sideways.

The troopers exited their cars. The one

trooper looked like he had papers in his hand.

I was a wanted nigga, and people up North,

including the Feds, would want to see me

locked up.

"Well, whatever you want to do. I'ma

ride out," Ra Ra said while setting his fork

down and now focusing on the troopers.

Ra Ra pulled out his 9mm and took off

the safety. He then placed the gun to the side

and covered it with the cloth napkin. We had

a corner booth by the bathrooms which

allowed us to see anyone coming and going.

"Listen Ra Ra, if I have to lay these niggas down, I will. I'm already wanted for killing a cop; the only thing they can give me is the death penalty, so one more cop ain't going to change shit. This is why I live like I do, because tomorrow isn't promised."

"I'm all in, homie. I can't turn back on all that you gave me and my homies. Blood in, blood out," he said, which is why I fucked with these ATL niggas.

The troopers approached the counter and made small talk with the waitress before placing the stack of papers onto the countertop.

"Have you seen this man around here?"

the trooper randomly asked. The waitress was an older woman looking to be in her late forties or early fifties. You could see she was a bad sista when she was younger, but now she was just a working mom. She looked over the photo and saw that it was me, but she didn't act like she knew me. Maybe it is a good thing that I always tipped her big. One time, I came in a little buzzed up and left a $500 tip. It was leftover money from the strip club I didn't spend, but it helped her out a lot, and she made me know how much she appreciated it.

"I never seen him before, but can I get you gentlemen anything?"

"No ma'am," he said before turning to leave.

"I'll be out. I have to use the bathroom," one of the other troopers said while making his way back to the bathroom.

He made his way into the bathroom only to see that the one-stall bathroom was in use, and he needed to shit.

"I got to take a shit!" the officer said with urgency.

Hearing that this muthafucka wanted to take a shit pissed me off. I ran into the bathroom to hide in the stall, hoping to evade them niggas. I tucked my .44 Magnum on my waistline, and then I flushed the toilet acting like I was taking a shit. As I opened the door to the stall, I was holding my hand on my stomach.

He glanced at my face as I passed him. He took a step toward the stall at the same time his brain was processing the image of my face. In that same moment, he turned toward me as it all came to him.

"Hey!"

I could hear his voice trying to form the words that would cause chaos and problems, so I turned toward him faster than he could get the words out. I was just in time to see him reaching for his sidearm. I beat him to the punch with the Magnum in hand, with the hammer cocked back all in the same motion.

The trooper knew that all the stories he heard of me were all too real. Today could have easily been his day, and he would never make it home to his family.

"Get on your knees and don't try to be a hero. If you know me, then you know I kill would-be heroes."

"I, I got two kids. Little girls. Please don't kill me," he begged, knowing the reality of this situation that he put himself in.

"It's too late for begging, you stupid muthafucka. You didn't think about your kids when you decided to turn around, did you?" I said, seeing the deep fear in his eyes. He was probably wishing he called in sick today to be with his daughters. "Slide your set of cuffs over here and the radio, too. I don't want you trying anything stupid."

I then made him wrap his arms around the pole going into the ground that held the stall together, before I cuffed him to it. I put the other cuffs on his feet, after he put them close to the other pole, so he was cuffed from both ends.

I left the bathroom and spared his life. I walked over to the table where Ra Ra was still eating his breakfast. Then it hit me. I couldn't leave him alive, so I took the steak knife from the table and made my way back into the bathroom. The trooper was attempting to escape.

"Look at what we got here. Are you trying to get away to get home to your daughters, or you trying to get me?"

I didn't wait for him to answer. I just took the knife across his throat, cutting deeply into his neck and leaving no chance of him seeing tomorrow. He started choking on his own blood as he struggled to suck in the much-needed oxygen to live another day, but it was too late.

Ra Ra stuck his head into the bathroom.

"My nigga, his partner is coming."

My adrenaline spiked, knowing it was

about to go down. Should I shoot it out with

this muthafucka, or what?

I turned to the urinal and acted like I was

taking a piss. I could hear the door open and

his partner's voice come through the air.

"Hey, Jim, we have a call."

Before he could even turn the corner to

see his partner dead on the floor, I came

behind him and slit his throat. He instantly

reached out for his neck and then his gun to

fire on me. But I grabbed his wrist and stared

deeply into his eyes.

"Just let it happen. Today is just one of

those bad days. It'll all be over soon," I said,

knowing he was dying and would not see the

sunset.

This nigga's blood got on my sleeve, so I rolled that shit up after I washed my hands. I wrapped the knife up and tossed it into the trashcan.

I calmly walked out of the bathroom, but Ra Ra knew what had taken place. He could see the murder in my eyes because he too was a stone cold killa with baby-face swag.

"Let's get the fuck up out of here. Leave baby girl a rack," I said, knowing she held me down.

After they discovered the two officers in the bathroom, she'd be trippin' on that shit. She smiled upon seeing the amount of money that Ra Ra handed her. She could take her kids out shopping or something.

Once we got in the parking lot, we got our shit together, and then Ra Ra raced off in his whip with the fifteen bricks I blessed him with. He was feeling himself being a young boss while I left town for a bit.

Me and Ra Ra really clicked since I had a baby with his sister, Candy. She was a firecracker but sexy as ever, standing five foot one and weighing 120 pounds in all the right places. She was the first piece of Atlanta pussy I got when I came down here. Light skin, long hair, glowing brown hazel eyes, sexy lips, and a soft voice that lured you in.

Our son was two and half months old. My little nigga's name was Dequan Jamir Anderson. We called him DJ for short. He had the world just like the rest of my seeds.

I made my way up North to take care of some other business. The good thing about driving alone was that it gave me time to think and really collect my thoughts, so I could stay ahead of the game and these cops that wanted to take me down.

# CHAPTER 5

**CLOSE TO TEN HOURS** later, I landed in my second favorite city: Baltimore, a.k.a. Charm City. It was also less than an hour from my home city of Harrisburg. It was like a home away from home. I got a suite at the Renaissance Hotel and Resort by using my fake ID. I booked the parlor suite. Room #7038 boasted a living room, dining room, and bedroom with floor-to-ceiling windows, giving me a view of the harbor and skyline. Once I got into the room, I hit up Rico from York, PA, who was only about thirty minutes away.

*"Nola que tal, quien es ese?"* Rico said after answering his phone.

"Now, nigga, you know my Spanish ain't on point like that," I said.

"Yo, bro, I know this ain't my boy America's Most Wanted," he said, trying to be funny, but excited to hear from me.

"Yeah, it's me. What you getting into tonight?"

"I don't know yet. Damn, bro! It's been a year, and you got at me just like you said you would. This shit is crazy."

"So, how's life been treating you and your team?"

"It's all good now, thanks to you. You

55

should see how we've grown."

"I'm up North and wondering what you and your team are getting into tonight?"

"We getting this money out here."

"Like I said, I'm close by, so meet me at Norma Jean's down the way, you feel me?

"I already know where we at with this. I'll be there around ten or eleven."

"I'll see you then, my nigga."

After the call with Rico, I called up my baby momma, Shari, in Harrisburg. She gave it to me right away, not hearing from me in awhile, but it was needed.

"Why did it take you so long to call? Don't you think your boys wanted to hear from you or know that their daddy is okay?"

"I know, I know, but things got a little more busy than I expected, plus I needed to secure myself," I began. "I want you to bring our boys down to the place with the dolphins, so we can see the show."

She got excited knowing exactly where I was.

"I'll be there around two."

"Sounds good to me. Plus, I got your favorite suite, too."

She giggled as memories flashed back to her of how we made love in every way in the suite. After the call, I made my way down to the gallery to get some new clothes for the week I'd be here, plus I needed something to stunt out with tonight.

"I'm hungry as a mutha right now!" I said, placing a quick order over the phone with the hotel staff for room service. I also ordered a few drinks to start my day off.

As I was waiting on my food, I flipped through the channels and watched CNN, which was showing coverage of the two troopers killed at the Atlanta Waffle House. The report said there were no suspects or leads thus far. This was good since I killed them both, because they would make the city hot for me. Fuck them cops. I turned to BET and watched videos on the 106 & Park. They started playing 50 Cent's video "Many Men"

with G-Unit. I stood up waving my gun and

feeling the moment and lyrics. In the middle

of the song, Ra Ra hit me up on my phone.

"What's good, little homie?"

"You see that shit on the news?"

"I seen it. We good, so keep hush on that,

feel me?"

"You ain't gotta tell me. I already know

the life we living," Ra Ra responded before

hanging up.

I was always paranoid needing to let

niggas know what they needed to say and do

at all times, so we could all be on the same

page at all times. Plus, some niggas thought

just 'cause you got away with something, you could tell everyone. That shit would only get you caught.

It didn't take long before my food came. I answered the door with my gun in hand until I looked out of the peephole. I grabbed the food, paid the staff, and then returned to the table. I dug in and drank my Long Island before I got ready for the fun tonight with my Spanish niggas.

# CHAPTER 6

**I JUST FINISHED UP** at 10:00 and got my gear together. I put on some Polo Black to smell good, along with my three-carat diamond necklace, two-carat studded earrings, and iced-out Breitling. I wore white linen pants and shirt, with butter suede 310s on my feet. I was looking like a superstar. I made my way over to the strip clubs on Baltimore Avenue, looking on at the swarm of people making their way to the clubs and restaurants. I turned down the little street where Norma Jean's strip club was located, and then I parked my whip across the street from the club. I gave the parking attendant a $50.

"Keep an eye on my shit, and make sure nobody bumps into my whip," I said, leaving the sky-blue Range Rover with him to look after while I balled out inside the club.

I entered the club looking like new money with a clean-shaven face, fresh cut, and with my diamonds doing the rest as the club lights bounced off of them and made them sparkle. The strippers all noticed my entrance as they were trained to do, meaning they clocked the money so they knew who to work to get their paper. I respect their hustle, which is why I love strip clubs.

I approached the bar and saw they also

had a bad-ass light-skinned chick working the bar, too.

"Let me get a Long Island and a stack in ones."

The strippers saw the stack of ones being placed on the bar along with my drink, so their eyes followed me back to the booth I sat in the back. This thick-as-a-muthafucka Asian stripper came over to me looking sexy in the face with just-right thighs that led to the curves of perfection in her ass. She came up with a smile of seduction as she asked, "Can I dance for you tonight?"

I smiled back thinking and saying, "Damn, baby girl, I was going to ask if I could dance for your sexy ass."

She laughed knowing my words weren't game but real talk. She knew she was exotic and different from the normal strippers. Atlanta had bad chicks, mainly thick sistas and some thick white chicks, but Asians didn't flood the clubs.

"What's your name?"

"Laila," she said, turning her ass to face me while doing her thing.

I caressed her ass with the stack of ones. It felt good to her, knowing that she was going to get some of it.

The crazy thing was that another exotic chick came up and looked like she could change a man's mind. She favored Olivia, the singer from G-Unit, with an exotic twist and a look of innocence. Her brown skin looked smooth like her silky black hair that lay over her perky breasts.

"Laila, sit on my lap, superstar!" I asked, to which she obliged as I gave her $100 in ones.

"You want to tip me for my dance?" the brown-skinned beauty asked.

"I didn't see you dance, but you are more than welcome to join me and Laila after you tell me your name."

"La La is what they call me around here."

"Now, La La, you can dance," I said,

taking another $100 from the stack and placing it into her red thong. She turned and smiled at me as she started popping her booty, dancing salaciously.

Laila was slow grinding in my lap while nodding her head to the music and playing with her hair in between looking back at me with her sexy bedroom eyes. She was also licking her lips like she could work them just as well.

"What are y'all two drinking?" I asked, knowing they get a commission from each drink I buy for them.

"Get me an apple martini," La La said as she bent over and touched her toes while twerking. A hell of a view from here.

"I'll take a shot of peach Cîroc," Laila responded.

I waved over another girl who I saw taking orders. She came back quickly, so I tipped her a $20 bill. As I enjoyed these two strippers, Rico and his team of Flaco, Chino, and Angel pulled up outside.

Rico pulled into the parking lot in his cocaine-white CLS600 Mercedes Benz that was sitting on 22s. There were televisions throughout with the Maybach curtains in the back window.

Flaco was right behind him in his 760Li BMW sitting on 23s with TVs and a PS3 all concealed behind the tinted windows.

Chino was behind him in his cocaine-white Audi S8 Quatro with the V-10 engine tricked out on 22s with low-pro tires, dual exhaust, and the chrome package throughout.

Last but not least, the youngest of the crew, Angel, drove up in his cocaine-white Bentley GT coupe with a black leather interior that was sitting on 23s and covered in tinted windows. He also had a custom alarm system just like the others. They all got the same color paint, feeling the image of this cocaine game that got them the cars. Plus that shit looked crazy when they all came through together.

All of their whips were parked side by side. Chino saw my whip, but he did not know it was mine. Still, he gave it props, loving the sky blue. Sky blue is my way of paying respects to Turnpike Tito, since he always said the sky's the limit.

They all came in stunting hard. They were all blinged and swagged out and looking like a different crew than before. I could see they made good use of the money that I left them with. They definitely made it work. Rico ordered drinks for his team as he looked around for me.

"La La, go tell my Spanish homies who just came in that I'm over here," I said, after seeing that he hadn't spotted me yet.

She did just that and strutted her sexy ass up to them. She pointed in my direction. I raised my glass, so he could see where I was sitting, 'cause sexy ass Laila, was sitting on my lap.

They came over without question. Laila got up and allowed me to embrace the homies.

"I see you looking good, bro, especially with the sexy China you with," Rico said after embracing me as he got an eyeful of Laila's exotic beauty.

"Y'all niggas look real good. I see y'all did well with that paper."

"We owe our success to you, bro," Chino said, pointing at the clothing and diamonds they were wearing.

"No, I owe y'all for making shit happen so I could be where I am today," I said. "Take a seat while my new lady friends go get some bottles. La La and Laila, get each of us a bottle of Cristal," I said, taking out three stacks and handing them to her. Each bottle is like $450 in the clubs. "Y'all split the change."

Right then they realized I was a boss nigga that wasn't from around here. They didn't have too many niggas like me coming through spending heavy bread this early in the night.

As they headed to the bar to get the bottles, it allowed me to have a conversation with my Spanish homies.

"So how are things going for you and your team?" I asked.

"Good, bro. We doing real good now," Rico responded as the girls made their way back over.

"La La, after you pass out the bottles, sit on my lap. Laila, you can sit your sexy ass right here," I said, making both women smile and feel good about being in my presence.

More strippers then came over upon seeing that my Spanish homies were all about the paper, too.

I leaned over and spoke to Rico as the music played loudly in the club. We then started talking business.

"So, what numbers are you getting at?" I asked, getting straight to the point.

"I get it at 18 a pop. I do seven to ten bricks a week."

"Not bad!" I said, thinking about when I was getting it for 13. "I can get it to you for a lower price; plus, what I'll do is front you twenty on top of the ten you buy to keep you busy for awhile. Can you handle that much?"

"With my team and the way, we think now, we can take over my city and this state,"

Rico responded.

"All right, I'll get it to you for 15.5 a pop.

Plus, this shit is high grade from my Miami

folks."

"I'm ready whenever you ready, bro."

"I'll get at you tomorrow with the details.

Now toast to a good night and an even more

lucrative future," I said while raising my

bottle of champagne.

Now I just had to figure out how I was

going to get the fifty bricks I left in my one

stash house over a year ago. I owned the

house through a family member to protect

myself. I also could use this cocaine to build

up my empire down in Atlanta. With these

two teams, I could grow and take over the East Coast. The thing was, I told myself I could never go back to Pennsylvania for anything. It was just not a good way to stay on the run with me going back to the place I was running from.

# CHAPTER 7

**WE ALL MADE OUR** way outside of the club at 2:04 a.m. Laila and La La also followed me knowing that I was a boss, and they wanted more than my money. They were looking for a good night and a possible good life that I could provide them. My little homies also came out of the club with exotic chicks ready for the hotel life. The party after the party.

"I knew that was your whip, Tommy," Angel said, after seeing me hit the unlock on the truck as the lights began flashing.

"I see y'all really stepped it up too, little nigga. I'm loving the cocaine-white theme, too. It's boss shit," I said, proud of the Spanish niggas. "La La and Laila, get in the truck. I need to holla at the homies real quick."

"Rico, we can make millions with your crew. I got these Fed muthafuckas tracking me; but with the right team, I can lay all the way back as y'all make the moves, feel me?"

"You already know we about our money and word. We stand behind you 100 percent. No matter what city or state you in, we coming to you to take care of this business, bro."

"Yeah, Tommy Guns, we owe you all of our loyalty to the end," Flaco said.

I knew these Spanish niggas were the real deal just like my little niggas down South.

Rico and his team left back-to-back, stunting on this city in their whips as they made their way over to the Hyatt on Light Street. I took the two exotic pieces back to my suite.

Once in the suite, La La and Laila were feeling the layout as well as the views of the city and the harbor that boasted million-dollar yachts.

"This is some balla shit right here, Tommy," La La said while walking through the suite.

"La La, check out this big-ass bathroom,"

Laila said, after seeing the Jacuzzi-style tub and the dual shower off to the side with jet sprayers for a full body massage.

The 30-inch TV added to the bathroom's luxury, but what stood out and impressed me was the phone by the toilet. Now that was some boss shit for when a muthafucka was taking care of a business deal on the toilet. Laila and La La were loving the suite as well as loving the fact that they had come across me. Both of them were so excited when they stood by the floor-to-ceiling window and took in the lit-up skyline of the city and the harbor with its yachts. I stood at the minibar pouring the ladies double shots of Hennessy

V.S.O.P before I then walked over and stood in the middle of the two Baltimore beauties.

"Here's a drink for y'all," I said as I handed them their drinks.

I then cupped their asses as they downed the double shots, feeling the warmth of the cognac roll down their throats.

I turned to Laila and lifted up her shirt, exposing her pretty nipples that my lips found with ease. At the same time, I took her ass in both of my hands, allowing my fingers to find their way under her miniskirt. My fingers slid into her tight wetness, which sent a stream of pleasure into her body that allowed light moans to escape her mouth.

"Mmmmh, I like that," she let out.

La La got wet and horny watching me and Laila, so she took her clothing off and then tapped me on the shoulder.

"Bring the fun over to the bed," she said while crawling onto the bed and displaying the art of her beauty as well as a level of intimacy. She looked back over her shoulder with her ass up and pussy open, looking wet and pretty. "Both of y'all can come get it," she said in the sexiest voice that would lure any man in.

I picked up Laila with my fingers still inside of her warm pussy while still making her moan as I carried her over to the bed. Her face and lips were pressing against my neck.

"Mmmmmm, I want you inside of me so bad," she whispered into my ear, kissing me on my neck.

Hearing this made my dick rock hard. I laid her on the bed and began to remove my pants. Laila wanted my dick bad, so she assisted me in taking my pants off. As soon as they came off and my boxers were removed, my dick was engulfed by the warmth of her mouth.

"Hold up! Let me lie down so we all can join the party," I said while lying on my back to allow La La to sit on my face with her pretty pussy, which smelled sweet as if she used a sex lotion to make her pussy taste real good.

I put my tongue and fingers to work, forcing a pulsating sensation through her body that made her moan and gyrate her hips as if riding my tongue.

"Mmmmh! Damn, your tongue is crazy. Aaah, mmmmh!" she let out.

Laila's soft lips were working her magic on my dick, which made me even hornier. Her soft hands assisted in stroking me up and down, with her tongue gliding over my dick and making it throb with each stroke.

"Oh my God! Bitch, his tongue game is real. Mmmmh, aaaah!" she moaned again, leaning in while trying to embrace the wave of pleasure surging through her body as my fingers and tongue moved in sync.

Laila stopped sucking my dick only to mount me. She took hold of my dick and rubbed it on her already wet pussy, and then she slid down on it. I ain't going to lie, right then I started feeling like I was going to erupt, but I held on. Her pussy was tight and wet at the same time, and it felt so good. She was feeling the same while thrusting her tightness up and down on me and feeling my dick all inside of her, which was sending erotic sensations racing through her body.

"Yes, mmmmh, yes! Mmmmmmh, I like

this big dick, aaaaaah, aaaah!" Laila let out,

riding me harder and harder, feeling my dick

pounding her spot and setting off a wave of

orgasmic sensation surging through her body

fast. "I'm about to cum, yes, yes, aaaaah,

aaaah!"

Her words and moans turned me and La

La on because La La started cumming on my

tongue as I continued working my fingers and

tongue. At the same time, I could feel myself

about to bust. My heart was racing as my

stomach tightened up. La La's motion in her

hips picking up as her body was releasing the

flow.

"Tommy, Tommy, your tongue is so

good to my body. Mmmmmh, damn, damn!"
she cried while breathing heavily.

I was about to cum and could feel that shit
rushing through my body each time Laila
went up and down hard on my dick.

"Yes, yes, yes, aaaaaaah! I like this big
thing!" she cried out, feeling her body letting
go of the orgasmic sensation that felt so good.

At the same time, I busted all up in the
tight Asian pussy. In the same instance, she
could feel me splashing inside of her. So she
started clenching her pussy to bring her up
and down motion to a halt as she slow ground
on my dick, taking all of my sperm into her
soft, warm wetness.

La La got off my tongue and kissed me. She loved her own juices, like it turned her on or something.

"Damn, Tommy, you got gifts," La La said with a smile. "Laila, you better get you some of this," she said while pointing at my mouth.

Laila was still releasing herself and having a crazy orgasm. She looked over her shoulder since she was riding me in reverse.

"You need to ride this pole and feel like I'm feeling right now," Laila said, before getting off of me.

The girls leaned in and kissed one another, touching each other's breasts and stimulating their bodies even more. Their fingers found one another's wetness while thrusting fingers inside. La La'a head went back as she let out an intense moan.

"Ohhhhhh, mmmmh!"

Hearing and seeing this shit got me brick hard all over again.

"Let me show you how my tongue works!" Laila said to La La, laying her back on the bed and parting her legs.

She then went into her love cave, allowing her tongue to meet her soft, wet pussy lips. Her female touch immediately sent orgasmic sounds into the room.

"Ohhhh, mmmmmmh, you good, you

good, mmmmmmh!" she let out, with her legs shaking, never having her body touched by another female in this way, so it enhanced the orgasms that she was having. "Aaaaaaah, aaaah, mmmmmh."

Her legs tensed up, and she was unable to stop the soaring sensation of orgasms rushing through her body. I started kissing La La in between sucking on her titties, adding to the pleasure she was feeling. Her heart, mind, and body were overwhelmed by the sensation and activity she had never had done to her body. Laila stopped her tongue play and came up to look at La La with a smile.

"You like that, too?" she asked.

"Y'all just tag teamed the shit out of my pussy, but I'm loving both tongues," she responded, still feeling her body releasing.

She became quiet and embraced the flow, until I got on top of her to stick my dick up in her super-wet pussy. I put her legs up and went deep. She took an even deeper breath before letting out more moans.

"Aaaaah, mmmmh right there, mmmmmh! I like it right there!" she screamed out, feeling my dick hitting the side back wall over and over.

Laila lay to the side popping herself watching me put work in on this pretty pussy.

"Mmmmh, mmmmh! Ohhh, I'm cumming, aaaah!" she moaned as my pace picked up and I slammed my dick into her harder and harder, side to side, and deeper and deeper.

I could feel myself about to bust, too, since her body was feeling so good. I let her legs down and allowed her to wrap her legs around me as I dug deep.

"Right there, mmmmmmh!" she let out with her lips and mouth pressing up against my ear.

The sounds of her moaning alone made me bust inside of her. She could feel me cumming as I pounded harder and faster. I came to a slow stroke, feeling good about these two bad-ass chicks and the night we were having so far. Life for me was good. This boss shit right here was what niggas upstate looked forward to when they came home. This was the same shit niggas rap about.

"I hope you're not done. I want some more of this dick!" Laila said, after lying off to the side still popping herself.

"We got all night, baby girl. We even can fall asleep, do breakfast, and start all over again," I said, ready for whatever.

At the same time, I knew they would be gone before I took care of my business with Rico and his team.

# CHAPTER 8

BY 11:00 A.M. THE next morning, after the long
sexual night I had with the strippers, I got up
quick and acted like it was check-out time.
They didn't need to know that I had the suite
for a week. As much as I would like to keep
them around for the week, their time was up.

"La La! Laila! It's time to go. Check out
is in an hour," I called out, waking them up.

They both got out of the bed slowly.

"We not leaving without getting a
shower," La La said.

"Take a shower then," I said, looking at
both of them walking naked to the shower

while thinking about last night and the fun we had. "I would come in there with y'all, but I'll leave ya to do the lady thing before I get clean."

"You going to miss out on the morning fun," Laila said while slapping La La's ass and smiling as they entered the bathroom.

I could hear them giggling as the shower turned on. As they showered and played with each other, I called housekeeping, so they could clean the room and change the sheets after the girls left.

Twenty minutes passed by, when the girls came out of the bathroom fresh and ready for the day ahead. Once they got dressed, I gave each of them a stack, not for their pussy but because I was a boss nigga. Besides, I might come to this city again and link up with these chicks.

"Give me y'all numbers. Here's a little play money for y'all to have fun with," I said, getting a smile from each of them for appreciating me and being in the presence of a boss.

"We love yo swag, Tommy. I hope we can do this again sometime soon," Laila said, leaning in for a kiss on the lips.

"Yeah, thank you for the money, too, and the good tongue and dick," La La said, giving me a kiss and then touching my dick. "Make sure you keep this tucked away until you come back to this city," she said with a smile before exiting the room.

Laila gave me a look like she didn't want to leave, and I didn't want her to go, but it was time for business. "Be good to yourself, all right?"

"Ain't no other way to live," she said while strutting her sexy ass toward the door before turning to blow me a kiss. "It'll all be good until we see you again."

Both of the girls was the truth and sexy as hell. I'll definitely hit them up when I get around to it.

I had to shower up and get fresh to death

for the day ahead. I also didn't want any traces of a female in the suite, which is why I had housekeeping come clean the room. I didn't want war with my baby momma when she came to the city.

# CHAPTER 9

**DOWN IN ATL, RA RA** was over at his sister Candy's crib eating a soul food breakfast of catfish, cheese grits, biscuits, scrambled eggs, and home fries with hot sauce and an ice-cold 22-ounce Colt 45 straight out of the freezer. A cold beer is always good to chase a good meal down with.

"Candy!" he called out while stuffing his mouth. He wanted to give his sis props on the food. "Yo, Sis, this grub is hitting."

He continued to enjoy his morning breakfast until time passed and his sis didn't join him as she planned. She had gone upstairs to check on his nephew. He stopped eating and listened in as if he heard something. Nothing. He stood from the table and took a swig of his beer to chase the food in his mouth, before setting it back down on the table. Then he pulled out his twin gold-plated 9mms that he just copped the other day. It was fully loaded, with one in the chamber and sixteen in the clip. Originally, he got them for show, but show didn't keep him safe, he thought.

With the safety off, he proceeded toward the living room, now feeling even more paranoid than before because Candy never responded to him when he called out to her.

As soon as he entered the living room, out of the corner of his eye he noticed someone was there, so he quickly raised his gun and pointed it in that direction. The other gun was also being raised, showing this nigga that he was fully loaded with twin *niñas*.

How the fuck had this nigga gotten in here without me noticing? Ra Ra hated the fact that he got caught slipping.

"What the fuck you doing up in here, nigga?" Ra Ra snapped while still aiming at this cat.

"We here to take yo' money, fool," Ra Ra heard him say, which made him aware that there was more than one nigga in the crib.

Just as those thoughts came to him, the other would-be robber came down the steps with Candy at gunpoint. He had his arm around her neck. At that very instant, Ra Ra shifted the gun in his left hand toward the nigga who was gripping Candy.

"Do y'all niggas know what y'all done got yourselves into?" Ra Ra said, thinking about these bitch-ass niggas coming for his money. "You want my money, huh?"

Ra Ra saw that these niggas came with no mask, meaning they came to kill for the money, and he wasn't about to let that happen to him or his sister.

"Candy, don't worry about these punk-ass niggas. They came to get paid, and I'ma pay 'em," Ra Ra said.

In that split second, he fired off two back-to-back rounds from the 9mm in his right hand, sending slugs crashing into the face of the would-be robber, ejecting brains and bones through the other side of his head. He was killed instantly, leaving him with no reflex other than falling to the hardwood floor. Ra Ra then shifted his attention and two 9mms to the nigga holding Candy.

"Now I cashed your boy out. You still want to get paid or what?" Ra Ra said, being sarcastic and pissed off at the same time.

"Nigga, we came here to rob you. I still

want the money, nigga, or I'll kill your sister," the robber said, not realizing if he killed Candy, he was going to die right behind her.

Candy didn't panic, since she knew her brother was going to handle this even if it meant she would have to take a bullet in the process.

"All right, fool. You want my money, hold up," Ra Ra said, turning back and going into the kitchen.

He opened the cabinet where he put a bag of money with seventy-five racks in it. Then he came back into the living room.

"This what you want? This bread, huh?"

Ra Ra said, dumping the money out and then grabbing two $10,000 blocks and tossing it over to him. "You want to get money, right? Well, there it is."

At the sight of the money, this dumb nigga let Candy go to grab the stacks of hundreds. Candy was smart and moved out of the line of fire when she saw her brother taking steps toward the nigga with fire in his eyes. He squeezed the trigger and bust shots into this fool's body, dropping him and the gun he was holding. Upon seeing him hit the floor, Candy walked over and kicked the shit out of him.

"That's for coming up in my house acting

stupid."

"I got this, Sis. Go upstairs and get your son," he said, upon hearing the baby crying, since all of the noise woke him up.

But the nigga on the floor wasn't dead. He was breathing heavily and still trying to grab the money as if he was going to get a chance to spend it. Ra Ra leaned over him and placed the gun to his head.

"It's time to cash that check, nigga. It's payday!" Ra Ra said, pulling the trigger and killing him instantly.

Ra Ra called up Little D, Geez, and Fat Money as he put them on point to what had just taken place. He also told them to come over to his sister's crib. Within ten minutes

they showed up, rushing to their homie's aide

and making sure he was good. Little D came

into the living room and saw how Ra Ra dealt

with these niggas.

"Oh shit, nigga! You put in some work

over here," Little D said while leaning over

the dead body. "You won't be robbing

anybody else, nigga," he said, making

everybody laugh at how crazy he was.

"What would make these fools think they

can put work in on you anyway?" Geez

asked.

"Man, I never even seen these niggas

before."

"No one else is going to see these fools either," Fat Money joked.

"All right, y'all help me get rid of these bodies and clean this shit up!" Ra Ra said. "Candy, while we clean up here, go shopping or something for a few hours, all right?"

"You sure you don't want my help?"

"We got this. Go buy my nephew some stunna gear," Ra Ra said while hugging his sis before she left.

Once she rolled out, they got the bodies together and secured them in plastic and old sheets. They took the bodies and dumped them in the large Waste Management dumpster. Their bodies would end up in the landfill, burned with the rest of the trash.

As they continued to cover the trail of death at Candy's spot back up north in Baltimore, I was sitting across from the Baltimore Aquarium waiting on my baby momma, Shari, who was supposed to be here at two o'clock sharp. I was there early to be on point with my surroundings. I wanted to see if anyone was here setting me up, like the Feds or cops. I was basically on the lookout for anyone or anything that just felt wrong or didn't look right.

I finally saw Shari standing where I told her to meet me with my sons.

That survival hood instinct kicked in,

telling me that something was wrong. As this

feeling came over me, I noticed that the four

benches near Shari were empty the whole

time I was waiting on her to arrive. They were

now occupied; but that wasn't all: all the

people sitting were reading newspapers. Now

if that shit wasn't obvious or the Feds, then

there must be something very important in

those papers that was better than the view of

the harbor and all of its attraction. She got the

Feds or the cops to follow her. This meant

they knew I was there or they just followed

her to see if I popped up.

I went into the plaza by the Cheesecake

Factory. I used a phone in the restaurant to

call her phone, allowing it to ring one time before I hung up. After that, I got this little young buck I saw out there panhandling. I gave him $50 and gave him a message to give before I rolled out.

The young teen-aged boy walked up to my baby momma.

"Ms. Shari, he said he still loves you and the kids, but you should know he can't make it because of the extra company that followed."

The boy walked away not awaiting any response. He had done what he was paid to do, and now he headed off to spend his daily earnings. Shari knew exactly what the boy meant, so she wasn't mad. She would rather see me free than in jail and heading to death row.

The FBI saw the boy take off, so they rushed in and tried to get him. But he blended into the crowd at the Aquarium, so they turned to Shari to see what had happened.

"What the hell just happened?" the agents asked.

She was scared when she saw them, because she did not know where they came from or how long they had been following her.

"I don't know what you're talking about. I came down here to spend time with my kids."

"What did that kid say to you?" the agent asked, figuring the boy was a messenger.

"He was begging me for money, and I told him no."

Shari got into her minivan with her kids and took them to get something to eat, since they wouldn't be having the day as she planned it. It was a good thing she didn't tell them she was coming to see me. Now she would have to be careful and alert since the Feds were obviously following her. It was crazy because it'd been over a year, but they wanted me bad. I wanted my freedom just as much, so they had better not come un-prepared.

# CHAPTER 10

**I MANAGED TO SNEAK** back into Harrisburg at 2:01 a.m. while at the same time creep into the back door of Shari's crib. I headed upstairs and opened my boys' door to their room, just to get a look at them while they were sleeping. Damn, I really missed them. I closed the door and went into Shari's room. I covered her mouth as I woke her up, because I didn't want her to scream. She opened her eyes, and her heart was beating fast thinking the worst, like rape, robbery, or murder, until she saw my face. Then happiness set in as I removed my hand from her mouth.

"You crazy, Tommy. I thought somebody was trying to hurt me," she said before smiling, obviously happy to see me. "I'm glad to see you," she said while leaning in to kiss me. "I didn't know the Feds were following me."

"Don't worry; I was on point. You know they're going to tail everybody they think talks to me. Your phones are tapped, so be mindful of what you say and do. Don't let anyone know that I was here. I came to get the key to the other house," I said.

She already knew what that meant. It was to the stash house where I kept more money and work. She took the key off of her key ring and handed it to me.

"Be safe out there. I don't want to see you all over the news dead or something."

"I got this under control. I love you and my boys, all right? I got to go. I'll send for you and the boys," I said before kissing her once more and then leaving out the back door.

As I was exiting the back door, I could see headlights from a car coming through the alleyway, which got my attention right away because it was so late at night. I ducked down low when I heard the car come to a slow approach. It was those boys. I could tell from the Crown Vic they were driving. They stopped at the back of her house and stared up at the house. No doubt they could see a light was on, on the second floor.

The one agent checked his watch and saw that it was 2:22 in the morning. Shari had gotten up, since she was unable to go back to sleep after seeing me, the love of her life. She had become emotional when thinking about how everything had unfolded with me and the Feds. How they wanted me dead or alive. She didn't want our kids to lose me.

As I was lying low, so as not to be seen in the dark, one of the agents took out his flashlight as he asked the other agent, "Did you see that? I think I saw something moving."

"I didn't see anything. Maybe you need a cup of coffee or something to be alert," the other agents replied.

I was still lying low in the dark shadows of the night as these idiots got out of their car with flashlights in hand and walked toward the back of the house. I pulled out my .44 Magnum ready to put these muthafuckas down. My heart started pounding while thinking about how this was about to unfold with each step they were taking toward the house.

Suddenly their attention shifted quickly as the one agent yelled out, "Oh shit!" A black alley cat jumped out and alarmed the agent's presence.

"Really? You got me out here tracking down alley cats? Wait 'til they hear about this back at the office," the agent said, busting his partner's balls.

They headed back to the car, not realizing they were ten feet away from a gunfight with me.

"Stupid muthafuckas don't even realize how close they was to dying," I said after leaving the yard.

I looked back up at the house and saw Shari in the window with the light on. She blew me a kiss through the air. I nodded my head in acknowledgment before I left. I then

headed to the stash house to secure some

bricks and a little more cash.

# CHAPTER 11

**THE NEXT MORNING I** was back at my suite sleeping when my cell phone woke me up at 9:45. It was my nigga Rico, from York.

"What's good, Rico?"

"*Que pasa*, bro? What happened to you yesterday?" he asked.

"Shit got crazy with them boys watching my folks, so I had to make a move around them to secure my situation and stay ahead of the niggas, feel me?"

"So everything *esta bien*, right?"

"We still good, my nigga. Meet me inside the plaza by Phillips buffet, and we'll go from there."

"I'll be there by noon, and we can get some of those crab legs and shit."

"Say no more."

I hung up and got myself together to take care of this business. I feel like my stay here up North is over with. It's time for me to go back down South with my ATL niggas.

At 11:05 a.m., back in Harrisburg at the FBI headquarters, Agents Smith and Johnson were focusing on tracking me down since they came up short when attempting to pick me up at the county. But those fake-ass agents showed up instead.

They knew the closest they were to me

was at the harbor, but they couldn't really prove it. They had agents sitting on my mom's crib and Shari's spot, too.

"Okay, everyone, I need you guys to listen up," Agent Smith began as he waited on everyone to look his way. He held up a picture of me. "It has been over a year, and this vicious cop killer is still out there. Either he's smarter than us, or we're simply not doing our jobs, ladies and gentlemen," he said before he paused and then scanned the room to see if he had everyone's attention. "He's getting comfortable. We know he reached out to his kids' mother," he said, not really having solid proof or they would have locked her up. "All family members we know of have taps and surveillance on their locations. We can't let him keep slipping through our hands as if the people he killed didn't matter. I want a full circulation of this photo as well as a computer-generated image of what he may look like now, with hair and no hair in the photos. It's time we brought him in. He's running and we're chasing him," Agent Smith finished, allowing his agents to get back to work.

Rico arrived at precisely 12:02 p.m. at the plaza. He didn't see me right away because I was in position to see who else came with him, just like I did with Shari. I came up behind him and tapped him on the shoulder.

"Be aware of your surrounds, my nigga,"

I said to fuck with him.

"I'm always on point, bro," he laughed.

"Let's go over here to Phillips' take-out."

Once we were by the take-out area, we

ordered food and drinks and then got straight

down to business.

"Oye, I got 155 for ten blocks. So with the

dub you blessing me with, I'll have to get you

3-1-0, which shouldn't take long if the

product is as pure as you say it is."

"Grade A, my nigga."

"Plus, I've been networking even more

knowing we got to step our game up," he

said.

I was feeling his drive knowing we could make millions together, especially with my ATL niggas.

"When you get done with this, we'll step it up to another level. It can only get better from here. Make sure you have baby bro Chino and Flaco handle business so you can be the boss of your city and up North, feel me?"

"I'm on the same page you on, bro. Longevity is key to this game."

"Once we done here we going to handle this BI, and I'll drop the product on you."

I told him where to meet me to get the

work. As we started leaving the plaza, I saw Maryland state troopers exiting their cars, but me and Rico were already leaving as they were coming our way.

"Yo, Rico, I'll see you in twenty minutes," I said so he could go his way.

I needed to get my truck out of the valet parking at the hotel, which was the same direction the troopers were coming. I turned back around and attempted to go back into the building, until the trooper called out.

"Excuse me, young man!"

My entire body tensed up knowing it was about to go down. I pushed my shades up on my face and adjusted my fitted hat that kept me concealed from prying eyes. I turned around to see what they had to say. He held out the picture.

"Have you seen this guy here?" he asked.

He was more focused on seeing if I recognized the person in the pictures rather than looking at me, which was all good.

"Never seen him," I said, after placing my hand over my mouth as if I was thinking about it.

"Thank you anyway. I guess the Feds got us on a goose chase," the trooper said as he and his partner made their way inside of the plaza.

That was the craziest shit ever to happen

to me in all my life. This muthafucka had asked me if I had seen myself, not even realizing he was showing the wanted picture to the wanted man. It was a good thing I was preparing to leave this city. It didn't take long before I cleared the suite, checked out, and then headed down the highway to see Rico.

His car was parked just where we discussed. The cocaine-white CLS600 Benz stood out, so I pulled up behind him. We both got out of our whips at the same time. I had to show him the flyers that the troopers were passing out.

"Check this shit out."

"That's you, bro."

"The troopers we seen gave it to me and asked if I seen that nigga."

"Oh shit, that's funny as a muthafucka. You don't look the same with the hat pulled down, shades on, and a clean-shaven face. You incognito right now."

"Let's handle this BI so I can get out of here," I said as I headed back to my whip to get the work. Rico went to get his money.

As I was reaching into the back seat of the truck, I noticed a car pull up behind my truck. Not good. I reached for my .44 Magnum snub nose and popped out the cylinder to see if it was fully loaded—and it was. I turned with the gun concealed behind the bag and approached Rico's whip to let him know these niggas just pulled up, and it didn't look right.

"Yo, you see them niggas that just pulled up in that black Nissan Maxima 3.5 SE?"

"Yeah, what the fuck are they doing?" he asked, which let me know he didn't fuck with these cats like that, so it was about to go down.

These niggas were either following me or him. Either way, I wasn't about to let them get the drop on me. So I set the cocaine in Rico's trunk that he had just popped to get his TEC-9 fully auto with a thirty-two clip with one in the chamber. Shots suddenly came through the air. I turned quickly and ducked behind my truck while closing in on these stupid muthafuckas.

I noticed that the driver didn't get out, so I aimed at him, sending thunderous slugs through the windshield that snapped his head back with brute force. His neck was broken as bullets violently entered his skull and killed him instantly.

The passenger saw his boy's brains all on the headrest, so he jumped out quickly. In that split second, my hood instincts told me to turn around. Right then, I saw this nigga Rico raise his gun and point it at me. Everything seemed to slow down in that fraction of a second or two as my mind raced while trying

to process this ultimate betrayal. Instantaneously, as these thoughts entered my mind, my finger started squeezing the trigger and unleashing thunder as the .44 Magnum let fire and fury go slamming into Rico's car. The slugs shattered his back window and driver's side door that he had opened, before he turned and jumped back into his car and mashed the gas. At the same time, I hurried and put in a speed loader and fired off more shots at his car that was racing away, causing him to swerve as I knocked out the front window and taillight.

All I could think about right now was

murdering that nigga and his whole family. But first it was time to kill the other nigga who had come with him. I came around the truck behind this nigga that thought I was still focused on Rico. I placed my gun to his head. In the moment, he thought he could turn around fast enough to beat me to the draw. I squeezed off, twisting him and his body back around before he dropped to the ground.

"You is a stupid muthafucka trying to take me out of the game," I said as his body hit the ground, before I fired off another shot into his head out of rage.

Then I dumped into my truck and mashed the gas, allowing the V-10 engine to thrust me down the highway to see if I could catch

up to this nigga Rico. His whip was faster and

he already had the lead, but I had my anger.

Within a few minutes, I realized I couldn't

catch him, and I figured his team was riding

behind him anyway, so I called up my ATL

nigga, Ra Ra.

# CHAPTER 12

**"ATL'S FINEST!" RA RA ANSWERED** the phone.

"Yo, my little nigga, I need you to get the squad and come up to PA. This nigga tried some bullshit."

"Say no more. We on the next flight," Ra Ra said before hanging up the phone to call the rest of the crew.

He called Geez, knowing the five-foot-ten, two hundred-pound thug was about his BI. Geez was a dark-brown-skinned nigga wearing the 360 waves and light sideburns that shaped up his baby face.

Then he called up Fat Money who stood

five foot eight, weighed a husky 230 pounds, and was always eating while riding around getting that paper, which is how he got his nickname.

Little D was the youngest of the squad who stood five foot five. He had an explosive demeanor that made him appear to be six six. He was only eighteen, but he was a fast learner and a ride-or-die little homie. He always rocked the braids, so the chicks he dealt with loved playing in his shit. He was light skinned with good hair.

Ra Ra was in the hood waiting on his team to come through, so he sat on the hood of his BMW M6. Fat Money pulled up first in his new all-black S55 AMC Mercedes Benz tricked out with custom features and the chrome package.

"What's good, Ra Ra?" he asked while stepping out and giving him dap.

"The homie called sounding urgent about something that went wrong up North, so we got to fly out ASAP."

Just as Ra Ra dropped the news on Fat Money, Little D and Geez could be heard driving up as they revved the engines on their Hiabusa 1300ccs they copped for fun, speed, and power. They both came through popping wheelies, trying to outdo the other. They let the bikes down and came to an abrupt stop by

Fat Money's whip.

"Yo, Little D, you look like you was about to hit my whip, fool."

"I got this, shawty," Little D said.

Ra Ra then explained the situation to them as he did Fat Money.

"If we going up there, how we going to get on the plane strapped?" Little D's crazy ass asked.

"We ain't, fool! He's going to have shit for us. You think he don't got folks with guns to sell up there?" Ra Ra said. "So if y'all ready, we at the airport now."

They jumped into their cars and drove away as Little D and Geez took off behind them on the bikes.

Once on the highway, Ra Ra and Fat Money opened up their fast cars. When Little D and Geez saw this, they opened up their bikes and did a comfortable and easy 140, passing Ra Ra and Fat Money, who were already doing 120 with ease. But they were no match for the bikes.

"Damn, them muthafuckas is fast!" Ra Ra said, seeing the bikes coast past him and Fat Money.

"I gotta get me one of them!" Fat Money yelled out when he saw his homies breeze by.

It didn't take long before they all made it to the airport. Fat Money and Ra Ra arrived after Little D and Geez, who were already posted up and waiting on them to get there.

"About time!" Geez said. "The cars look good for the ladies, but when it comes to getting away or going somewhere, these bikes is where it's at."

"Me and Money definitely getting bikes when we get back. Now let's get our tickets," Ra Ra said.

As they boarded the plane to head to Harrisburg, I was back in the city myself. I needed to come back to secure some things. I was riding heavy with twenty of the fifty kilos I had grabbed from the stash house.

I made my way deep into the hood. The

Southside projects were known as the South Acres, and for the mass violence that occurred out there. One thing I did know was that cops really weren't for chasing niggas through the rows of projects. That shit could easily be a setup.

The hood was alive with everybody cooking out, partying, and playing with water hoses for the kids and adults that just wanted to cool down. Niggas were blasting the music from their cars.

I came through looking for an old friend from before I went on the run. He was someone I knew was a gun runner in the hood and other cities.

As I was coming through the projects, I could see this classic old-school 1976 Boxville Cadillac with gold spokes, two-inch white walls, and a rag top that made the candy-apple-red paint job pop. The boom-erang on the trunk also set it off. My old friend was drying the Cadillac. I pulled up to the side of his car.

"Move that piece of shit!" I said fucking with him, getting his attention too, since everybody in this hood knows who he is and what he's about.

Cash is his name, Dominican born, with a bald head. He stood six foot two, weighed a fit 225, and wore a full beard that was cut close.

Upon hearing me tell him to move his car, he started to reach for his gun on his waist-line, until he raised his head and saw my face.

"*Como amigo*, you almost got yourself shot. *Que pasa, mi hermano*? I know you didn't risk coming back here to look good in that truck," he said, knowing I was on the run.

It was stupid for me to be here, but my plan was to be in and out.

"Urgent business. I need to deal with a problem I have. Enough on that. How's the BI treating you?"

"Business is moving, but not as fast as I would like it."

"Well, I'm here to spend," I said, getting his financial attention.

"Park your truck right here and follow me," he said.

I did just that, and then followed him into his crib. As we walked to his house, he nodded his head to his lookouts, so they knew to be on point and alert him if anything went down. They knew to secure the crib front and back, so no one could go in or out without Cash being present. Once in the house, he locked the doors behind him.

*"Hermano, que to quieres?"*

"I need something that's going to make this muthafucka realize he shouldn't have run off with my thirty bricks."

"*Ahi Dios mio, hermano*. I feel sorry for the person you're after," Cash said while making his way into the closet to grab the green military bag full of guns.

He came back into the room and lay out all of the guns on the floor. He definitely had the heat. He had ARs, H&Ks, MP5s, AKs, and a crazy selection of handguns. What stood out was the 10mm Taurus with modifications, making the handgun fully auto when holding the trigger.

"*Tu gustan* anything, hermano?"

"I like all of this shit, but I'ma go with the 10mm Taurus. Give me two of them for myself. Let me get two of them ARs, six Glock 40s, and extra clips for all of the weapons."

I pulled out a brick of the cocaine and placed it on the table. Cash looked at me like it was food stamps or something.

"*Espera un minute,* hermano. Cash only."

"The brick is worth more than the guns, Cash, and you know this. Plus, for supplying me with bullets, I'll give you another brick, and you'll be able to triple the cost of these guns."

He gave me this look. I knew that if we hadn't done good business before he would not have done it, plus he knew I was not going to ask for something unless it was important.

"I don't usually do the bullets for anybody, but I know you can't just go to Walmart or someplace to get this shit, so I'm going to do this for you, hermano. Besides, it's a great deal for me since business is slow. I'll have *mi primo* push this shit."

Cash put all the guns I ordered in a bag with the ammo, and then he turned and handed me the bag. "Don't come back, hermano, because you're hot and I don't need that around here. Besides, they'd deport me, hermano."

I laughed while acknowledging him.

Cash opened the door and stepped out. I followed behind him and walked back to the truck as he did the same before wiping his car down. I passed off the brick, and he tucked it into the trunk of his car.

"*Adios, mi amigo!*" Cash said as I pulled off.

As I was driving ready to leave the South Acres, I saw this nigga JD who originally introduced me to D.C., the undercover federal agent named Derick Corrnick. My blood started feeling like it was boiling, because this nigga right here was the reason I was on the run right now. He didn't see me or even know what type of whip I had, so the surprise was mine to own this moment.

I turned my music down to focus on the move I was about to make. I drove up past him and pulled into a parking space as I waited for him to walk by.

I pulled out old faithful, my .44 Magnum with one speed loader left.

"This skinny muthafucka is running these streets like snitching is cool out here," I said.

I was pissed off with every step he was taking. Especially with him walking out the South Acres, which was a hood that was known for its violence and gunshots all day and every day.

I let him walk past my truck before I got

out, which allowed me to be behind him.

"Yo, you bitch-ass nigga!" I said to get his attention. He turned around and saw that it was me. Like he was seeing a ghost, his eyes widened in fear as his mind tried to tell him to get the fuck out of here. "You set me up with that fake-ass hustla. That nigga was a Fed."

He put his hands up and covered his face as if he could stop the slugs if I fired on him. Suddenly, he realized that death would come to him if he stayed around. So he turned and ran away, but not fast enough. I fired off two roaring rounds that raced through the air and slammed into his flesh, flipping him in a forward motion that he was already going in.

I didn't wait around. I jumped into the truck and took off. I headed to the airport to meet my little niggas from the ATL.

Little kids from the hood came over to JD and pointed at him.

"Look! He's dead with all that blood," a seven-year-old boy said to his friends.

"Nah, he's moving," the eight-year-old boy said.

At the same time, JD let out a gasp, which scared the shit out of the kids, so they took off running. The sirens could be heard coming since someone called for the ambulance when they saw the downed man.

# CHAPTER 13

**I ARRIVED AT HIA** at 7:00 p.m., where I waited

for Ra Ra and the rest of the team to come out

of the airport terminal. This is the last place I

wanted to be, with all the heightened security

after Amir Hussein did that dumb shit like he

was going to blow shit up.

There's my little niggas, I was thinking,

after seeing them come through the doors. I

blew the horn and then rolled down my

window.

"Over here, little homies!" I yelled out.

They all came over and got into of the

truck. I drove off quickly. I wanted to head to

York to take care of this business.

"What's going down, Tommy Guns?"
Little D asked.

"These Spanish niggas I was dealing with
took me for thirty bricks. The crazy thing is,
these are the same niggas that broke me out
of jail. I blessed them with bread, so it don't
add up," I said, thinking this nigga Rico may
have been on some solo shit.

"We gonna ride with you no matter what.
But first, where's the heat at?" Geez said,
obviously talking about the guns.

"They're in the back. I got a few things
y'all might like, plus six Glock 40s and
plenty of ammo."

Geez opened the bag in the bag and saw the twenty bricks.

"Yo, Tommy Guns, you got heavy block in this bag."

"Not that bag, the other one got that war-ready shit up in there," I said.

He found the bag and took out the guns.

"Geez, give me that one right there, the AR-15. I can put some work in with this shit," Fat Money said while removing the clip. "Give me a box of bullets," he added, all ready to load up.

"Geez, hand me one of them ARs and a box of slugs. Me and Money are going to terrorize shit!" Ra Ra said.

Little D and Geez took two Glocks a piece with some extra clips. I already had the twin 10mm Tauruses with extra clips and ammo.

"Yo, Tommy, you know where to find this nigga that did that dumb shit?" Fat Money asked.

"Yeah, right now he'll be over at his sister's crib with the work. By now he probably called up his little brother and homies. I want y'all to know they ain't going down without a shoot-out, so stay fully loaded and don't hesitate to kill these niggas. Because they will take you out," I said, wanting to make sure my ATL niggas made it back home, because I would feel bad having them come this far not to make it back home.

"It's whatever, big homie. We came here to take care of business," Little D said, all hyped up and ready to hang out.

The homies all loaded their weapons as I put on a CD from my hood nigga, Large Flava, a.k.a. Big L. He was a DJ who put out hits and also played local artists' material like this one now by Kaotic Da General. The song "Bang" featured Blackass, another artist from Harrisburg. All these guys were representing hard through their lyrics and lifestyle.

At 8:04 p.m., back at the hospital in

Harrisburg, Jason D. Dawight, also known as JD, was laid up in the bed from his wounds. He still feared Tommy Guns, who he deemed the face of evil. Tommy Guns figured JD was dead from the two powerful slugs that tore through his body, but this fool was like a cat with nine lives. JD assisted the Feds in taking down Tommy Guns and his cousins with their drug ring, but now he was feeling as if he was back in the same position as before with this crazy muthafucka looking for him. He didn't realize that Tommy seeing him was pure coincidence.

Now the Feds were standing over him wanting to know what he knew. This was especially true since the nurses said while he was in and out thinking that death was coming to him sooner than later, he kept saying "Tommy Guns is a devil. Tommy did it."

When the nurses heard this, they felt a need to contact local law enforcement, who reached out to the Feds.

"JD, he came for you, and now he'll come again," Agent Johnson said. "I just got back in town today. How the hell did he know I was here?" JD questioned them, with fear in his eyes.

"If that's the case, then it means he was in town for other purposes, and you just so happened to cross paths. It's called karma. You did set the guy up."

JD couldn't believe he was hearing this shit. I know what the fuck karma is, he was thinking.

"So, what does he look like now?" Agent Johnson questioned.

"The devil. The fucking grim reaper. How the hell am I supposed to tell on him now, when he came back and shot me? As you said, karma. So, what now? I can't take too many more bullets. This shit hurts," he said while pointing to his body with the exit wounds from the slugs.

"We're going to put you into witness

protection. No one will be able to get to you.

But if you tell us what he looks like now and

what he's driving, this could help bring him

down, and you wouldn't have to worry about

witness protection," Agent Johnson said.

The room fell silent from voices, other

than the beeping machine that displayed his

heartbeat and rhythm. However, the silence

was broken as he described Tommy to a T

and explained his features and weight loss,

down to the vehicle he was driving. The Feds

were all over this information, sending it

back to headquarters so the other agents

could be aware. It was also imperative to

make the other agencies aware of his new

look. In the meantime, they had someone watch JD's room until he got better, and then he would go into the witness protection program.

This would be the life that JD would now have, since he chose to be a rat. Too bad Tommy Guns' bullets didn't kill him. Now Tommy would have another problem that he was not even aware of, with the Feds knowing his description and vehicle.

# CHAPTER 14

**AT 9:31 P.M. I** was sitting in my truck in York with my Atlanta niggas down the street from Rico's sister's crib watching the traffic. I remembered the address from when we were out in the county together. He gave me her info to contact him along with the number that I used when they got me out.

With the traffic in and out, it was making me think that this nigga was selling my shit. I noticed Chino's car was parked in front of the house. Rico's CLS600 Benz was there, too.

"What up, Tommy Guns, we ready to lay

these fools, or what?" Little T said.

I was processing the moves we needed to make so everything could go in sync, so we all would make it back down South.

"Yeah, we ready. Ra Ra, you and Little D hit the back door. Fat Money, you come with me. Geez, you cover the front door. Nobody that ain't us comes in or out," I said as I exited the truck.

They followed suit doing the same and taking their positions.

Inside of the house, Chino and Rico were looking at the bricks on the table, taking it in and seeing that they had just come up. Rico was snorting from a mini mountain he had on the table beside all the bricks of cocaine.

Chino was also snorting the cocaine. He was

high as a muthafucka.

"Oye, this is some grade-A shit. He

wasn't lying about that," Rico said, touching

his face and feeling how it became numb

from snorting the cocaine.

"We going to be rich, bro," Chino said

while looking at all of the cocaine and taking

another snort of the raw.

"Yeah, we gonna get this money, and the

fiends is going to love this shit!" Rico said,

drinking his Corona to chase his high.

"Did you tell Flaco or Angel about this,

bro?" Chino asked.

"Nah, I couldn't tell them about this move, bro. They respect Tommy Guns for the love he showed us. I do, too, but we needed to make this move, bro, to pay Dominican Manny in New York," Rico said.

He was spending money faster than he could make it, which left him owing a violent drug kingpin in New York, Manny, who took the city over after King Jose died.

"Bro, you telling me you fucked up all of your money?" Chino asked in surprise because they all were living good.

"I was living crazy with all the trips to Vegas, Atlantic City, and Miami, as well as the women, the clubs, and the cars. You

know, bro, so don't judge me. I fucked up!"
he admitted, now feeling regret for doing
what he did robbing the big homie.

"Fuck it! We here now, bro, and we got
the *yayo*," Chino said while snorting another
line. "*Cono*, this is good shit!" he said, tilting
his head back and taking it all in.

A knock at the door got their attention.
Rico covered up the cocaine while Chino
went to answer the door. He could see it was
a young buck that hung out with Rico's
nephew.

"*Es Pito aqui?*"

"Nah, he ain't here right now."

"Are you sure he's not here?" the boy

asked, pissing off Chino, who tried to look past him being nosey. "My mom said I can stay the night."

"Come back in like thirty minutes. He's not here right now. I'll have him call you."

"Okay, don't forget," the boy said as he walked away.

Chino closed the door, but within a few steps away from the door, he heard another knock.

"He better take his bad ass home," Chino said while opening the door again.

As the curse words toward the little boy came out of his mouth, I swung around with the twin 10mm Tauruses and fired on him. He didn't even have a chance to alert anyone in the house. By the time his body hit the floor, the young boy had taken off, while I made my way into the crib and walked past Chino's lifeless body.

Rico heard the roaring of the gun and grabbed his MAC-11. Geez still covered the front door while Fat Money followed me inside with the AR-15 ready for war. Rico came in fast, charging into the living room and firing off rounds until Fat Money unleashed the AR-15 that forced him to retreat back into the other room.

"You fucked up by coming here, Tommy. You know my team ain't going for that!" he yelled out as he was dialing up his brother.

~ ~ ~

Flaco picked up on the second ring, hearing the gunfire erupting in the background.

"Bro, where are you?"

"Over at Carmen's crib. These niggas are trying to rob me," he lied to his brother before he hung up.

Flaco told Angel what was going down, so they raced over to Carmen's house and parked halfway down to the street. They thought they'd try to get the drop on whoever was in the crib.

Flaco was strapped with the AK-47,

while Angel boasted the 9mm Uzi as they approached the house ready for war.

~ ~ ~

An all-points bulletin was sent out for me at 9:45 p.m., with a new description and vehicle. The FBI also warned all law enforcement, "Tom 'Tommy Guns' Anderson is extremely dangerous. Approach with caution and guns drawn."

"Rico, I'm going to kill you, muthafuckas! I gave you and your team life in this game! If I had time, I would torture your sister, too, nigga!" I said, pissed and ready to take care of business with this nigga.

As I yelled out, Ra Ra and Little D kicked

in the back door, which placed even more fear into Rico when he heard the door breached.

"Oye, punta! I'm going to kill your amigos. I hear them coming!" Rico said, aiming his gun toward the kitchen entrance and firing off a burst of rounds halting any entrance from that area. That shit only made Little D and Ra Ra want to kill his ass even more.

Rico recklessly fired another burst of rounds in my direction, sending slugs into the walls and furniture. Then I heard the clicking sound of an empty gun. Rico knew he had to think fast, so he looked over to where Chino's

body was lying and saw his gun by the table
with the bricks of cocaine. Right then he ran
toward the gun. That's when me and Fat
Money sprayed bullets, hitting him in his ass
and legs and back-dropping him.

"Ahi Dios mio, cabron!" he yelled out,
feeling the hot slugs burning his flesh.

We closed in on him, leaving him no
chance to grab the gun and return fire.

"You stupid muthafucka, I gave you and
your team a jump start on this game, plus I
was blessing you with the bricks, and you did
that dumb shit!"

"I fucked up, but what's done is done,
cabron. Shit happens!" he responded, know-

ing the end was near.

"You right, shit does happen!" I said, squeezing the trigger and marring his face as the bullets tore his left side off and killed him instantly.

"Yo, Ra Ra, you and D sweep back out the back door. Money, you come with me," I said, upon seeing the stack of bricks partially covered up. I secured the coke. That's when I heard gunfire erupting outside. Geez was shooting out with Angel and Flaco.

"Toma! Toma! Toma!" Angel yelled out, letting the AK-47 rip.

Ra Ra and Little D came around just in time to ambush the Spanish niggas, chopping down Angel and Flaco and dropping them as slugs filled their backs.

I was coming out of the house fast, ready to roll out and make sure my homies were good. I came up and saw that Angel was still alive, but he was barely breathing and trying to speak when he saw my face.

"Oye, Tommy! Que pasa, bro? I thought we was cool!"

Right then I knew this little nigga didn't have anything to do with it. But he wasn't about to let my team just kill his brother and be good with it, so he had to go too.

"Your brother and his homies in the black Maxima robbed me and tried to kill me earlier."

Angel heard this and knew who the men were. But he couldn't do anything about it, because his brother was on some sneaky shit that cost his team their lives.

"*Lo siento*, bro. That fool fucked up a good thing!" Angel said, knowing the end was now here for him.

I didn't kill him personally, giving him that much respect. I walked away, and Little D finished him off.

"Yo, get the keys off of that nigga right there. He won't be needing that BMW," I said.

They got Rico's keys to his BMW 760Li

as Ra Ra and D jumped into the BMW.

"This is a crazy-ass whip right here, Ra Ra," Little D said while admiring the custom features and details.

We took off feeling better about getting the work back, but bad about having to kill Flaco and Angel, because they were real. We headed back down South before stopping in Fredericksburg, Virginia, to get some rest for the night.

# CHAPTER 15

**IT WAS 11:03 THE** next morning and time to check out. Me and the little homies were ready to head back down South with these forty-eight bricks. We were short two because these niggas probably sold them or got high, but there wasn't any telling.

As we came out of the rooms, I noticed two Fredericksburg police cars parked side by side by my whip. I didn't know if they were on a donut break or scoping my shit out.

"Yo, to be safe I'll drive the truck, my nigga," Geez said.

Fat Money followed Geez as I rolled with

Ra Ra and Little D in the 760Li BMW.

The crazy shit is that as we started walking away to the cars, the cops got out of their vehicles with pictures in hand. They then looked at Geez and tried to make a comparison of the image in the photo.

"Excuse me, sir, is this your truck?" the officer asked, still looking back at the picture again as if I and the little homie looked alike.

"Yeah, this is my whip. Why you asking?"

"You don't ask the questions, we do!" the officer snapped, now standing alongside the truck about three to four feet away.

Geez knew the AR-15 was in the back

seat, so he had to tone it down not to draw attention to himself.

Ra Ra started the BMW as we all were concealed behind the tinted windows.

"What questions are you asking, because I have places to be and people to see."

The officer took another look at the paper before walking to the back of the truck to check the license plate. At the same time, he grabbed his radio, so he could run the tag.

"Ra Ra, drive up behind these fools, so I can make sure the homies are good," I said, upon seeing this idiot walking to the back of the truck.

I was sitting in the passenger side, so it

gave me a good view of what was going on as well as access to these stupid assholes.

Ra Ra stopped the car right behind the officer, which made him halt what he started to do. He still had the radio in his hand. I hit the switch that made the dark tinted windows roll down to expose my face to the officer looking in my direction. His heart jumped when he saw the vivid comparison of the picture he was holding in his other hand.

"Looking for me, muthafucka?"

Before he could respond or alert his partner, I did what I had to do. I squeezed off a round into the center of his forehead and ejected his brains out the other side as the brute force of the slug threw his body up against the truck, leaving his lifeless body to slide down the back of the truck. The other officer reacted and reached for his sidearm, but Geez swung two hard punches back-to-back, knocking the cop out cold. His whole body went stiff from the powerful punches that crashed into his chin.

"Night, night, nigga!" Geez said while looking down at the cop.

"You, Geez, and Money go grab the coke and the rest of the bullets. We gotta get the fuck outta here before that nigga wakes up," I said. "Ra Ra, hit the trunk so they can put that shit in there."

As soon as they got into the whip, Ra Ra mashed the gas and raced off with ease as the powerful V-12 engine pushed us down the highway while we were making our escape.

~ ~ ~

The front desk clerk inside the hotel heard a gunshot, so she walked outside and found the two downed officers. One was dead, and one was out cold. Not knowing who had done this, she called it in, fearing the worst for herself and the guests.

Five police units showed up within a minute; some even faster since they were in the area. Immediately, they all took notice of the blue Range Rover Sport and connected the dots between the dead officer and the downed officer. Once the other officer came to, he updated them on what had taken place and how everything happened faster than he could react. The lead officer knew right then that he needed to contact the FBI since their wanted man had killed one of their own.

"Agent Smith speaking."

"Mr. Smith, this is Officer Roberts down here in Fredericksburg, Virginia. Sir, we found the truck that you guys have in the picture. It has the Atlanta tags. And let me tell you, that son of a bitch killed one of my men. I tell ya, if he's still around here, he's not going to make it out of Virginia alive,"

Officer Roberts said, feeling the pain of the loss of his officer.

"Officer Roberts, there will be agents on the scene after I hang up. I'll be down as soon as I can."

"I reckon I'll see ya then."

After the call, he and the remaining officers secured the area with yellow tape.

~ ~ ~

Back on the highway, the BMW 760Li was coasting down I-695 and assisting in our getaway.

"Geez, you knocked that muthafucka out! I bet he didn't see that shit happening!" Little D said all hyped up.

"I didn't know what else to do. Y'all couldn't shoot him because he was standing too close to me and I didn't have a gun. So, I did what fear told me to do—knock that nigga out!" Geez said laughing.

As they talked about what had taken place, I closed my eyes and lay my head back on the rest, thinking about all that had taken place over the last few days. Shit truly had been crazy in my life and around it. I was now actually feeling the pressure from these Fed niggas as if the end was coming. The crazy thing was, at this pace, it felt like I wouldn't even be able to stop that shit from happening.

# CHAPTER 16

**WE WERE BACK IN** Atlanta two days later. At 5:00 a.m. Ra Ra and Fat Money were still sleeping in the living room at Candy's house. They both had passed out the night before after drinking and playing PS3. They were still on point, however, since they fell asleep with their weapons at their side, especially after them niggas tried to creep Ra Ra for his money.

~ ~ ~

Outside of the house, federal agents were closing in with hopes of taking Tommy Guns down. They had traced the Range Rover's tags back to Candy's house since it was in her name.

A still silence fell as the agents synced up to breach the house. They woke up Fat Money and Ra Ra with a flash-bang grenade that came through the window and shattered the glass. This was followed by the loud boom and bright light that briefly disoriented them, giving the agents enough time to kick in the front and back doors. In that instance of being abruptly awakened, both men zeroed in. They took hold of their weapons and quickly fired off at any moving target, not even allowing the agents to announce themselves. Because at this point, the flash bang and doors being kicked in were more than enough announcement. The AR-15 slugs were unforgiving, killing the first agent through the door. Body and head shots pierced the vest, not that it mattered with the head shot.

Ra Ra and Fat Money realized it wasn't a robbery but the Feds. Now knowing they had just killed a Fed, they briefly looked at one another and knew the only way out of this was with gunfire. In other words, they would go out fighting until death, because jail was not an option.

The agents returned fire after being caught off guard. They did not expect to enter a gunfight, because they felt they had the advantage of entering the house in the early morning hours with the flashbang. They felt the men would panic and surrender, but the opposite occurred.

Ra Ra's eyes saw the shadows of more agents outside of the window as if they were attempting to come through the window, so he fired off more shots in that direction and forced the agents to shift their direction of entry.

The agents by the door pulled the dead agents out of the house, knowing they were at a disadvantage with the men being where they were.

Silence fell once the gunfire ceased, which made Ra Ra and Fat Money even more paranoid. They looked around with their guns aimed at the windows and doors. They were ready for whatever.

A voice came from outside of the house. It was an agent trying to get their attention.

"You men in the house! My name is Agent Smith. I'm with the FBI. We came here to talk to Candy Smith about her truck!"

"You should have thought about talking to her before you kicked the muthafucking door open, making a nigga think we were getting robbed!" Fat Money said.

"My sister ain't home anyway. Plus, it's

too early for you to be coming here talking and shit!" Ra Ra yelled out.

While Agent Smith continued talking, agents managed to get into the house.

"You're right, my friend, it is too early. But as you can see, we can't leave now. You killed two of my guys. So, we have a big problem!"

"First off, you ain't got no muthafucking friends in this house! As for the 'we' thing, we don't have a problem, since we'll kill the rest of y'all!" Ra Ra said.

Fat Money then made the move by closing in and firing rounds through the window. At the same time, agents were climbing through the second-floor windows,

so they could have another angle of attack.

Fat Money was so paranoid that he swept his

gun back and forth. Right then he caught

movement out of the corner of his eye. He

saw someone creeping down the steps. He

shifted fast and fired the AR-15 on the agents.

"I'll kill all of you, muthafuckas!" Fat

Money yelled out, with his finger pressing up

against the trigger and sending bursts of fire

through the air while lighting up the inside of

the house as bullets spit from the gun.

Fat Money started charging toward the

steps, killing the agent in front. As his body

fell down the steps, Fat Money was so

focused on adding a few more rounds to his body to assure his death, that he slipped on the agent that was backing the other agent up. He fired on Fat Money and hit him in the chest, legs, shoulder, and stomach, thrusting Money's body against the wall and dropping him and his weapon.

Ra Ra saw this and opened up, spraying the fully modified AR-15 to unleash the entire clip as long as his finger was on the trigger. He killed the agent that was focused on taking Money down. Again, the house and outside of the house fell silent as he rushed over to Fat Money, who was choking on his own blood. He was just seconds away from death.

"You going to be good, my nigga. Don't close your eyes. We got them. It's time to get out of here now," Ra Ra said, knowing his homie was near death. "Money, come on, man!" Ra Ra's voice broke, feeling the pain of losing his childhood friend.

Fat Money held onto life while gripping his gun.

A shot rang out inside of the house, coming from behind Ra Ra, that slammed into his side and shoulder and forced him forward. The crazy thing was that Fat Money's last gangsta moment of life was that he squeezed off a burst of rounds that crushed

Agent Smith's chest and skull, dropping him where he stood.

Fat Money was no more at exactly 5:45 a.m. His eyes were still open, but no one was in there. He lived like a gangsta and hustled 'til the end.

Ra Ra closed Money's eyes.

"I'll see you on the other side, my nigga," he said as he got up and headed into the kitchen to grab his bag of money that he kept in there.

It was quiet, so he looked out of the window and saw no one in sight. He slid out of the house wounded and got into his whip. Agent Smith didn't feel the need to bring more than the agents he had, because he figured he had the element of surprise. But his decision cost him his life as well as the lives of the other agents.

Ra Ra called Tommy Guns right away.

~ ~ ~

When I saw the number come across my phone that early in the morning, I knew something was wrong. Besides, it had been going that way lately anyway.

"What's good, Ra Ra?" I asked half asleep.

"Shit just got crazy at my sister's spot. The Feds came fast and killed Fat Money, but he went out with a bang. I'm hit up, too, but them Fed niggas is dead."

"Yo, shit is crazy. Go to the hospital and get right. Then come see me. I'll be on point just in case them Feds come my way."

"They may have traced the truck back to my sis. They acted like they was there to talk to her and shit."

"All right. Hit me up when you come from the hospital," I said before hanging up the phone.

I knew I couldn't go back to sleep after hearing some shit like that. Just like before the Feds got the full-court press on making me feel like the walls were closing in fast, I had a feeling that my time may be coming to an end, just like homie Fat Money. I was going to miss that nigga as real as he was.

# CHAPTER 17

**AT 11:05 A.M. RA RA,** Little D, and Geez were all at my hotel suite where Candy and I stayed overnight. But now with the call I got this morning, I knew I couldn't stay in this city any longer.

"Yo, Ra Ra, you feeling better now, my nigga?"

"I'ma make you know. Plus, I made it out of there alive and not in a jail cell."

"I got a lot of love for y'all ATL niggas. Y'all been holding me down since I came into this city, but it's time I moved on until the heat dies down. Ra Ra, you got to leave for awhile, too. So Little D, you and Geez have to take over the game and step it up," I said before I paused, thinking about the homie Fat Money going out like a G. "Geez, you and Little D take Money's mom one hundred racks for the funeral and his kids, and let her know that as long as we breathing, they good. Ra Ra, you have to head to the border, so how's Mexico sound for you?"

"I know a little Spanish from school, but I guess I'll have to pick it up even more now."

Candy came in between us to hug Ra Ra.

"I love you, Bro. Take care of yourself and don't get killed out there," she said, knowing how crazy that country could be.

"I made it this far in life, so Mexico is going to be low key."

Ra Ra gave his parting love to everyone before leaving and jumping in his whip toward the border.

"Geez, I'll meet you and D downstairs in a few minutes, all right?"

"We'll be downstairs."

Once they left, Candy embraced me. She was scared of me and her brother leaving. The fear made her horny, so we had a quick round of sex in the bed and in the shower. Once we were done, I kissed her goodbye and then made my way down to the homies standing by the stolen 760Li. I popped the trunk of the BMW, took out the bag of bricks, and handed them over.

"Here are forty-eight joints up in here, more than enough for y'all to take over and change the game in y'all's hood and more. I'll be back in a few months, but I'll still call weekly to see if y'all need anything."

"Be easy no matter where you land at, my nigga," Geez said.

"Yeah, we going to move this work in no time."

"Little D and Geez, be smart and move slow. It's how you last in this game, all right?"

"You already know!" Geez said.

I dapped the homies up before getting into the BMW and taking off, leaving this city I loved so much, along with the women and the realest niggas I ever met. I had close to two hundred racks, which was more than enough for me to do whatever I needed to do and stay low wherever I landed. Besides, if I needed bread, I would hit the little homies up for my cash flow or head back up North to my stash houses.

# CHAPTER 18

**THE FBI, LOCAL LAW** enforcement, and multiple
media outlets were all over Candy's house at
3:04 p.m. in response to the downed agents.
Agent Johnson was present after hearing that
his long-time friend had been gunned down.
It really choked him up, and he wanted to
avenge his brother in arms.

"They killed him. I can't believe they
killed him!" Agent Johnson said, torn apart
over his partner's death. "We have to take
these sons of bitches down that did this.
Death row will be the least of their worries!"
he added, displaying his anger as he started
kicking Fat Money's dead body as if he could

feel the pain he was trying to inflict on him.

"That's enough already!" Jack Ross's voice boomed through the air, upon seeing Agent Johnson acting out his emotions. "If you can't contain your emotions, I'll excuse you from this case."

"I'm good, I'm good," he responded vacuously.

FBI Director Ross felt a need to fly in after hearing about this atrocity. Sitting behind the desk or staying in the office would not suffice.

"I take it this is one of the goons that killed our agents?"

"Yes, sir. And from the looks of it, there were more men shooting, because one person would not have been able to take out these agents like this," Johnson responded, not realizing that was exactly what had taken place.

"I'm thinking there may have been one other shooter because there are two beers on the table over there. And from the looks of all the casings, they were the same as what our agents were using," Georgia Agent Jackson said.

"That's a good eye, Agent Jackson. I need this entire house swept for more answers that will lead to taking down those that participated as well as Tom Anderson," Jack Ross said.

Candy was just pulling up in a cab preparing to put on an Oscar award-winning performance as if she knew nothing about what had taken place. She got out of the cab and raced toward the taped-off yellow line behind which the media outlets were held along with the quidnunc neighbors.

"What's going on? Why y'all all in my house?"

The agent closest to the yellow tape stopped her from coming across it.

"Ma'am, calm down. Is this your house?"

"Yes! Yes! Is my brother okay?" she asked as she began to fake cry.

Candy stood a sexy five foot one and weighed 110. Her innocent hazel-brown eyes sparkled with lust when she was in the mood, but now they were flooded with fake tears.

"My name is Candy Smith."

Jack Ross came over after the agents made him aware of her presence.

"How are you doing today, ma'am?" Jack asked. "I'm Jack Ross, so this is your home?" he asked, wanting to get straight to it. Her tears meant nothing to him after he had lost agents. "This is Agent Johnson. We're here because my men are dead, because they came to serve a warrant for Tom Anderson who we believe was driving your truck that we found in Virginia," Jack Ross said as he led her and Agent Johnson back to the house and away from the reporters. "Where were you around five o'clock this morning, Ms. Smith?"

"I was at the Marriott Hotel."

"With whom?" Agent Johnson hurried to ask.

"With someone I met at the club last night," she quickly responded with a slight attitude.

"Does this guy at the club have a name?" he fired again, trying to catch her up.

"What the fuck is all of this about? Call the Marriott. They'll tell you who checked in and out," she fired back.

"Okay then. When is the last time you saw Tom Anderson, also known as Tommy Guns?"

"It's been awhile," she responded.

"How long is awhile?" Agent Johnson

questioned, not trusting her.

"A few months ago."

"How is it you're here in Atlanta, yet we found your truck in Virginia next to a dead officer?"

"What dead cop?" she asked, unaware of this.

"You said three months ago, correct?"

"Yeah?"

"So, he's had your truck that long?"

"He bought the truck for me but drove it the most."

"So, you didn't know he was wanted by the FBI?"

"No, I didn't do a background check on him or none of the guys I see," she responded.

"So, what do you consider yourself to him, collateral damage or what?" Agent Johnson said sarcastically.

"I'm the mother of his son."

"Ms. Smith, excuse us for a minute," Jack Ross said as he stepped away from her.

Candy stood thinking that she had fucked up somehow, but the Feds were really just temperature checking with her. Tommy Guns was their main focus, and also the person responsible for the deaths of these agents.

"Ms. Smith, come with us," Johnson said while leading her into the living room where Fat Money's lifeless body lay.

"Do you know this man here?"

Seeing his body dead made the reality of

what she already knew all too real. Her heart was feeling for Money, knowing he was a good friend to her brother and her.

"Yes, he's my brother's friend."

They didn't need to ask any more questions. They knew what they needed to do next.

"Thank you, ma'am. You can't stay here for awhile. If you have a place to go, I think you need to go there until we're done here."

"I'll go to my mother's house."

"We'll need that information, so we can stay in contact with you."

They walked Candy out of her house as the reporters swarmed her for information.

Once the agents came back inside, they

put out an all-points bulletin on Raymond

"Ra Ra" Smith for the murders of the agents

in the house. Now Ra Ra was on the run just

like his big homie Tommy Guns. They were

running for their lives and freedom. They

knew they could not look back, because a jail

cell was not in their future.

*The End ~ For Now*

***Part 3 Now Available***

***Text Good2Go at 31996 to receive new
release updates via text message.***

*To order books, please fill out the order form below:*
*To order films please go to www.good2gofilms.com*

Name: _____

Address:_____

City: _____ State: _____ Zip Code: _____

Phone:_____

Email:_____

Method of Payment:      Check      VISA      MASTERCARD

Credit Card#:_ _____

Name as it appears on card: _____

Signature: _____

| Item Name | Price | Qty | Amount |
|---|---|---|---|
| 48 Hours to Die – Silk White | $14.99 | | |
| A Hustler's Dream - Ernest Morris | $14.99 | | |
| A Hustler's Dream 2 - Ernest Morris | $14.99 | | |
| A Thug's Devotion – J. L. Rose and J. M. McMillon | $14.99 | | |
| All Eyes on Tommy Gunz – Warren Holloway | $14.99 | | |
| Black Reign – Ernest Morris | $14.99 | | |
| Bloody Mayhem Down South – Trayvon Jackson | $14.99 | | |
| Bloody Mayhem Down South 2 – Trayvon Jackson | $14.99 | | |
| Business Is Business – Silk White | $14.99 | | |
| Business Is Business 2 – Silk White | $14.99 | | |
| Business Is Business 3 – Silk White | $14.99 | | |
| Childhood Sweethearts – Jacob Spears | $14.99 | | |
| Childhood Sweethearts 2 – Jacob Spears | $14.99 | | |
| Childhood Sweethearts 3 - Jacob Spears | $14.99 | | |
| Childhood Sweethearts 4 - Jacob Spears | $14.99 | | |
| Connected To The Plug – Dwan Marquis Williams | $14.99 | | |
| Connected To The Plug 2 – Dwan Marquis Williams | $14.99 | | |
| Connected To The Plug 3 – Dwan Williams | $14.99 | | |
| Deadly Reunion – Ernest Morris | $14.99 | | |
| Dream's Life – Assa Raymond Baker | $14.99 | | |
| Flipping Numbers – Ernest Morris | $14.99 | | |
| Flipping Numbers 2 – Ernest Morris | $14.99 | | |
| He Loves Me, He Loves You Not - Mychea | $14.99 | | |
| He Loves Me, He Loves You Not 2 - Mychea | $14.99 | | |
| He Loves Me, He Loves You Not 3 - Mychea | $14.99 | | |
| He Loves Me, He Loves You Not 4 – Mychea | $14.99 | | |

| | | | |
|---|---|---|---|
| He Loves Me, He Loves You Not 5 – Mychea | $14.99 | | |
| Lord of My Land – Jay Morrison | $14.99 | | |
| Lost and Turned Out – Ernest Morris | $14.99 | | |
| Love Hates Violence – De'Wayne Maris | $14.99 | | |
| Married To Da Streets – Silk White | $14.99 | | |
| M.E.R.C. - Make Every Rep Count Health and Fitness | $14.99 | | |
| Money Make Me Cum – Ernest Morris | $14.99 | | |
| My Besties – Asia Hill | $14.99 | | |
| My Besties 2 – Asia Hill | $14.99 | | |
| My Besties 3 – Asia Hill | $14.99 | | |
| My Besties 4 – Asia Hill | $14.99 | | |
| My Boyfriend's Wife - Mychea | $14.99 | | |
| My Boyfriend's Wife 2 – Mychea | $14.99 | | |
| My Brothers Envy – J. L. Rose | $14.99 | | |
| My Brothers Envy 2 – J. L. Rose | $14.99 | | |
| Naughty Housewives – Ernest Morris | $14.99 | | |
| Naughty Housewives 2 – Ernest Morris | $14.99 | | |
| Naughty Housewives 3 – Ernest Morris | $14.99 | | |
| Naughty Housewives 4 – Ernest Morris | $14.99 | | |
| Never Be The Same – Silk White | $14.99 | | |
| Shades of Revenge – Assa Raymond Baker | $14.99 | | |
| Slumped – Jason Brent | $14.99 | | |
| Someone's Gonna Get It – Mychea | $14.99 | | |
| Stranded – Silk White | $14.99 | | |
| Supreme & Justice – Ernest Morris | $14.99 | | |
| Supreme & Justice 2 – Ernest Morris | $14.99 | | |
| Supreme & Justice 3 – Ernest Morris | $14.99 | | |
| Tears of a Hustler - Silk White | $14.99 | | |
| Tears of a Hustler 2 - Silk White | $14.99 | | |
| Tears of a Hustler 3 - Silk White | $14.99 | | |
| Tears of a Hustler 4- Silk White | $14.99 | | |
| Tears of a Hustler 5 – Silk White | $14.99 | | |
| Tears of a Hustler 6 – Silk White | $14.99 | | |

# ALL EYES ON TOMMY GUNZ 2

| | | | |
|---|---|---|---|
| The Panty Ripper - Reality Way | $14.99 | | |
| The Panty Ripper 3 – Reality Way | $14.99 | | |
| The Solution – Jay Morrison | $14.99 | | |
| The Teflon Queen – Silk White | $14.99 | | |
| The Teflon Queen 2 – Silk White | $14.99 | | |
| The Teflon Queen 3 – Silk White | $14.99 | | |
| The Teflon Queen 4 – Silk White | $14.99 | | |
| The Teflon Queen 5 – Silk White | $14.99 | | |
| The Teflon Queen 6 - Silk White | $14.99 | | |
| The Vacation – Silk White | $14.99 | | |
| Tied To A Boss - J.L. Rose | $14.99 | | |
| Tied To A Boss 2 - J.L. Rose | $14.99 | | |
| Tied To A Boss 3 - J.L. Rose | $14.99 | | |
| Tied To A Boss 4 - J.L. Rose | $14.99 | | |
| Tied To A Boss 5 - J.L. Rose | $14.99 | | |
| Time Is Money - Silk White | $14.99 | | |
| Tomorrow's Not Promised – Robert Torres | $14.99 | | |
| Tomorrow's Not Promised 2 – Robert Torres | $14.99 | | |
| Two Mask One Heart – Jacob Spears and Trayvon Jackson | $14.99 | | |
| Two Mask One Heart 2 – Jacob Spears and Trayvon Jackson | $14.99 | | |
| Two Mask One Heart 3 – Jacob Spears and Trayvon Jackson | $14.99 | | |
| Wrong Place Wrong Time – Silk White | $14.99 | | |
| Young Goonz – Reality Way | $14.99 | | |
| Subtotal: | | | |
| Tax: | | | |
| Shipping (Free) U.S. Media Mail: | | | |
| Total: | | | |

**Make Checks Payable To:**
**Good2Go Publishing**
**7311 W Glass Lane,**
**Laveen, AZ 85339**